THE CHOICE

Alice rose and came toward me.

"You'll get caught into it and then you'll wake up one day and say, 'What the hell have I done to myself? I'm trapped. And there's no way out anymore. The money is too steady and too good. The prestige. The power. The fawning people about me. My wife.'"

"What do you mean 'my wife'?"

She was standing over me. But now she turned and walked away to the edge of the deck and stood there gazing out over the water, saying nothing, absolutely nothing.

"I wish you'd see things my way," I said.

She didn't turn.

And I knew what she had meant. She would never be my wife. Never. Not if I took that road.

Someone else would be.

Other Avon Flare Books by
Jay Bennett

THE EXECUTIONER
THE KILLING TREE
THE PIGEON
SLOWLY, SLOWLY I RAISE THE GUN

I Never Said I Loved You

Jay Bennett

AN AVON FLARE BOOK

I NEVER SAID I LOVED YOU is an original
publication of Avon Books. This work has never before
appeared in book form.

AVON BOOKS
A division of
The Hearst Corporation
1790 Broadway
New York, New York 10019

First Avon Printing, April, 1984

AVON TRADEMARK REG. U.S. PAT. OFF. AND IN
OTHER COUNTRIES, MARCA REGISTRADA, HECHO EN
U.S.A.

Printed in the U. S. A.

WFH 10 9 8 7 6 5 4 3 2 1

For Frances
Ever in our memory

1

It had started to snow again. A long, thin, curling snow that fell silently to the ground. Slowly and surely covering it. I stood at the narrow window and looked out at the grey afternoon sky. Stood and thought and felt lonely and bleak. It was December twenty-eighth, the Christmas season, and I was not home but here at Princeton in my room. The part of the campus I could see from my window was wide and empty. Most everyone had gone away to families and friends, and I had stayed on in this small, two-storied dorm house. I had to rewrite a freshman term paper.

I stood there watching a lone figure walking through the snow, watching it until it was gone out of my view. And now all I could see was a cluster of bare and silent trees. The snow covering them with a thin, cold veil.

Endlessly.

After a while I began to realize that the phone was ringing: I stood listening to it; it seemed to come from another snowy world, a soft, distant ring. It kept on. Till I turned away from the window and went over to my little desk and picked up the receiver.

"Hello?"

And then I heard her voice.

"Peter?"

"Yes?"

It was from another world.

"It's Alice. Alice Cobb."

Another time.

"I know," I said.

And then I sat down.

"How're things?"

"All right."

"Your folks said you'd be here."

"I'm here."

"They said you had to finish a paper."

"That's right."

"What's the matter? Did you screw up?"

"Sort of."

"You've a good mind, Peter. You shouldn't do such things."

"I guess I just wasn't able to concentrate," I said.

"Oh."

There was a slight pause.

"How're things?"

"All right."

"You like it here?"

"Yes."

"Nothing like Westfield High."

She said it like a statement, not like a question.

"No."

"We're in the big leagues now."

"That's a good way of putting it."

"The pitching is better and tougher. They throw you a lot of fastballs."

"And a lot of curves."

She laughed, a low, gentle laugh, and I listened to it—deep underneath it there was a note of sadness. And then she stopped laughing and began to speak again in almost a rush of words.

"The big leagues. Wisconsin is the same. It can get awfully cold out there. Awfully cold. When I left for the Christmas vacation it was five below. Five below, Peter. And the day before it was three. Awfully cold."

"Yes."

I noticed that my palms were damp. I was listening to her voice, to every word she said.

"I should be used to cold. Come from Chicago. Grew up there. You know that."

"Yes, Alice. I know," I said.

"Should be used to it. But I guess I'll never get used to it. There are things one never gets used to. Isn't that so, Peter?"

"It's so," I said.

"It's not so cold here in Princeton, even though it's snowing. Just thought I'd call you. That's all."

"It's good to hear your voice, Alice."

"It's good to hear yours, Peter."

And then there was a pause.

"Where are you now?" I said.

"I'm at the gas station on Hopewell Road. Filling up my car and checking on my snow tires. I'm on my way back to Wisconsin."

"It's a long trip alone."

"Yes, Peter. It's a long trip."

And then she said, "But I don't mind."

She had come from Westfield, Connecticut. Westfield is on the Long Island Sound, and Princeton was not on her way out to Wisconsin. There are shorter and more direct ways to the University of Wisconsin—certainly not through Princeton, New Jersey.

But I said nothing. I noticed that my heart was beating rapidly. But I said nothing.

Then I heard her voice again.

"What time do you have, Peter?"

She never carried a watch.

9

"It's close to three, Alice."

"As late as that?"

"Yes."

"What's the exact time, Peter?"

"Why?"

"Just feel like knowing it. Sometimes I feel like knowing the exact time. You know that."

I didn't say anything. Yes, I did know that.

I looked down at my watch, and the flash of its gold band in the dim afternoon light made me think of the flash of her blond hair when she walked in the sun. The sun of spring.

"Four minutes to three," I said.

It was more of a honey blond. Honey blond. That's it, exactly.

"Four minutes to three. But it's no longer four minutes because time races on. It races on too fast for me." She laughed. "It's almost three minutes to three. And before I know I'll be twenty and then thirty and then...I hate what time does to people and things. Don't you, Peter?"

Then she laughed again, as if at herself, but again there was that sadness deep under her laughter.

I felt her sadness reach into me. And stay there.

Her father had given her a gold watch on her eighteenth birthday and she had lost it, almost at once. She lost a lot of things.

He got angry at her when she told him she had lost the watch. I was there when a lot of things happened to her.

"Peter?"

"Yes?"

"Are you still there? I've been talking to you."

"I'm here, Alice."

"You've been dreaming."

"I've been listening."

"Good. How about having dinner and then I'll be on my way again?"

"Dinner?"

"Just so we can catch up with each other. Find out what the world's been doing to you and me."

"Oh," I said.

And again I felt the surge in my heart.

"What about six?"

"Six?"

"Well?"

"I don't know, Alice," I said.

"Why not?"

"Just don't know."

"You mean you don't want to."

"I didn't say that."

"You don't have to."

"Alice," I said.

"Well?"

I didn't say anything. There was a pause.

"Well?"

I still didn't speak.

"Forget it. Sorry I disturbed you."

Now I wanted to say something. I never wanted to hurt her. She was always too dear to me.

I wanted to say something to her. But I didn't.

"Good-bye, Peter."

I heard a click on the other end and I knew that she had hung up.

"Good-bye," I said in a low, a very low, voice.

I sat there in the silence and looked at the wall and felt all closed in and not able to break out of myself, and then the phone began to ring again.

I picked up the receiver.

"Peter?"

"Yes, Alice?"

Her voice was brisk.

"You've been studying all day?"

"Sort of."

"Writing?"

"Yes."

"Since when?"

"Since early morning."

11

"How early?"

"Eight."

"I thought so. Then take a break. We'll make it ten minutes to six at the Princeton Inn."

I didn't speak.

"Ten minutes to six. Or six on the head."

And now I could feel a haunting anxiety come into her voice.

"Well, Peter?"

Back, back in her voice, so concealed that no one but I could detect it.

"Well?" she asked again.

"All right, Alice," I said.

"Are you sure?"

"I'm sure."

"You have enough money for your share?"

"I have enough."

"If you're short I'll pay for the dinner."

"Alice, you forget. You're the one who was always short of money."

"Oh. Was I?"

"Yes."

"I guess you're right, Peter."

"I'll see you at six," I said.

"I'm glad, Peter."

"I am, too."

"Are you?"

"Yes."

In the silence I could swear that she was holding back her tears. And she was not one to cry easily. It took an awful lot to make her cry.

"Alice?"

"Fine," she said in a cool tone. "I'll see you at six."

"At the Princeton Inn."

"The Princeton Inn, Peter."

She hung up.

And I knew that now she had begun to cry.

I sat there a long time, until I realized that the receiver was still in my hand. I slowly put it back into its place and then I finally got up and went to the window. It was still snowing. A cold, timeless snow.

"Alice."

My voice was low but it echoed through the empty room.

"Alice," I said again.

This time it was a whisper. A lonely whisper. And then there was silence, full and complete. I looked through the window at the white flakes sharp and clear against the grey sky.

And as I looked I remembered.

Remembered everything.

2

I remember, as the saying goes, the first time ever I saw her face. It was in Mr. Palmer's classroom and the sun was coming through the windows and outside it was spring. The class had already begun when she came into the room and went over to Mr. Palmer and handed him a note. He read it and then smiled at her and directed her to a seat, and the seat was just across from mine.

And that is how I first saw her face.

It made no impression on me then. I turned away from it and began to listen to the lecture on T. S. Eliot.

I used to like his poetry very much.

I don't anymore.

The class was on English literature. It was an advanced class for selected seniors, and Mr. Palmer went on for a while telling us how important and significant and influential Mr. Eliot was to English and American literature. A giant of our times.

He paused and then asked for questions and comments. And it was then that I first heard her voice.

And as I look back upon it, it was the voice that first drew me to her. Yes, it was that.

Low and warm and full of change. Slow balls, fast-balls and low sinkers. Like a pitcher who had a lot of stuff. And all of it good.

I know I'm not making sense. But did I ever make sense when it came to her?

She was speaking but I wasn't listening to her words, and then, when I saw a look come over Mr. Palmer's face and his lower lip begin to tremble in anger, I began to listen.

"...and so I believe that Eliot was a minor poet at best. That he was the worst possible influence on American writing. The worst. We're still not getting over it. But I'm sure we will. We're too smart to be taken in all the time."

Mr. Palmer drew in a breath and then asked quietly, very quietly, "The worst influence. Can you tell me why?"

And now her face was beginning to interest me.

"Because he saw hopelessness and despair for our world. Nothing but that. He was a self-centered aristocrat who had no real feeling for people. And a poet who has no feeling for people is not a poet. He's nothing then but an intellectual phoney."

"Your name?"

He knew her name from the note she had given him. But he was angry. Boiling with anger. And we could see that he was going to lose his cool. He had a reputation for being always calm and temperate.

"Cobb. Alice Cobb."

"You've just transferred to this school?"

He had been giving his T. S. Eliot lecture for twenty years already. It was an honor to be selected for his class.

"Yes."

"From where? May I ask?"

"Chicago. A high school in Chicago."

"I see."

15

He drew in his breath again and put his long, lean hand to his cheek and began stroking it, and we knew from that gesture that he was going to calm down.

"I see," he said again. "Quite enlightening, Miss Cobb. It was good to hear your comments."

He was giving her a chance to let things stay as they were. I thought she was going to sit down.

But she didn't.

"I think it's time Eliot was debunked. Once and for all. He's a dull and rotten poet. There's not a line of his that sings. He doesn't write poetry. He writes obscure junk."

The hand came away from the cheek and Mr. Palmer now stood tall and trim.

"It's quite evident that you feel very strongly about Eliot."

"I do."

"Is that by the way the prevalent attitude in Chicago high school courses on literature? I mean when it pertains to Thomas Stearns Eliot?"

"No. It's mine."

"Ah."

"Completely mine."

"You've read him, I'm sure."

"Every word I could stomach."

"Ah," he sighed.

"Every word."

He had blue eyes and they were frosty now. She had blue eyes and they were calm and steady.

"I see we're going to have an interesting term together, Miss Cobb."

"I see it also."

His head went back a bit.

"What were your marks?"

"I was an honor student."

"And your extracurricular activities?"

"I was president of the G. O."

"Among other things, I'm sure."

16

"There were other things."

He nodded and smiled, his frosty eyes studying her intently. And suddenly I began to realize that he was enjoying her. That he was glad she was in his class.

"It's going to be an interesting term together, Miss Cobb," he repeated wryly. "I see where we'll both be learning from each other."

She smiled now, and it was a warm one.

"I think we will."

"And now do you mind sitting down?"

"Not at all."

She sat down and was silent for the rest of the period. She took notes just like the rest of us did.

It was the last class of the day, and I followed her outside and into the sun. But I didn't say anything to her at all. Just followed her and watched how the sun played on her blond hair, making it glow.

It was only later on that I called her "Alice of the golden hair."

Only later on.

3

And I remember having an argument with my father that day. No, it wasn't over Alice. Those arguments came later on. It was over careers.

"Baseball?" he said, and dropped his fork onto his plate so that it clattered there. My mother looked across the table at him and tried to smile and divert him. She loved peace at all costs. This was her second marriage. Her first had blown up in her face and it had sort of traumatized her.

This was her second and she wanted it to be a forever one. It had been that way for a good twenty years now. A pretty good marriage. But she still couldn't settle back and enjoy it. I guess when life hits you hard you just never forget the jolt.

Yes, you never forget.

"Pete is not serious, Dan," she said.

"Of course I'm serious," I said.

I really wasn't but I think I did it just to get a rise out of him. Sometimes he cut to the bone.

I pitched for the high school team and we had won the all-state championship two years running. I had even had some nibbles from big-league scouts.

But he had never come to even one game to watch me pitch. He had absolutely not a shred of interest in baseball.

Squash was his game.

I guess he never forgave me for sticking with baseball and not taking up squash. I think he looked forward to having a lot of pleasure with me on the court.

He must've waited slow years for that pleasure and then I kind of screwed him up on that.

But he never said a word about his hurt.

He's a distant man, if you know what I mean. And I guess I have some of that in me, too.

When it comes to deep feelings, feelings that really count, he keeps a lot of it inside him. And that's what I do. And yet I know I care a lot about him, and that he, in his way, cares about me.

I think I'm on target with that one. I think I am.

"Baseball?" he said again. "What kind of a career is that in this day and age?"

"Lots of money in it. Lots of fun."

He raised his grey eyes to me.

"Fun? A grown man is supposed to have fun in his career? A career is your life's work, Pete. Work. I repeat the word. Work."

He was brought up that way. Ever since he was a child. It was drummed into him. And he tried to bring me up that way, too. Fall into a pattern.

I still don't know if he has succeeded. It's a toss-up.

"Why not have fun in it?"

"Fun?" he said. "You're supposed to go into law."

"Supposed?"

"Yes."

"Why?"

My mother waved her hand at him but he went on inexorably.

"What do you mean 'Why'?"

"Just what I said."

19

"Pete. Dan. Please."

"We'll take care of this, Ruth. Please."

He was a corporate lawyer and he did more than well. Every morning he got into a train on the New Haven Line, settled back in his seat, took out some legal papers from his briefcase and did not look up until the train pulled into Grand Central Station. Then he rose to his full height of six feet one inch, a trim and almost dapper man, slowly put away his glasses and walked out of the train, into the station, tall and erect, and then out of the bustling station and into a cab, which took him downtown to his Broad Street offices. Every evening he got off the train, the six-twelve, and my mother picked him up in our Lincoln and drove him home.

His father had been a corporate lawyer and his grandfather before him. So I was in line to pick up the tradition and go into that old, long-established firm.

My father had the office picked out for me. He had even showed it to me once. I was fourteen then.

Oh, another thing—very important. He was so busy with his career that he didn't have time to get married until he was thirty-five. And I was the only child of the marriage. After me there had been no time left for another child. They had both considered themselves too old to have another one.

So there it was.

And as I was arguing with him I knew that I was eventually going to do what he wanted. I would become a lawyer. A corporate one. Because that was the easiest way to go.

And maybe that's why I went ahead and baited him. Maybe out of a little contempt for my father.

And for myself.

Sometimes I used to say to myself, did he really want to become a lawyer, was that in the center of his heart, or did he finally buckle under the pressures of that hard and unbeatable tradition and just give in?

I tried to ask him that once when we were alone and kind of close to each other at the moment. But he shied away from it. Deftly. Like a wise old batter who won't be suckered into a bad pitch.

And I'm kind of the same way with him, when it comes to inner truths. I'm that way with everybody. You can get that close to me and then I move away from you. I told you we're kind of distant people.

The one who really got close to me was Alice. Yes, she was the only one.

"You've got a nice office for me in your law firm all set up. Haven't you?"

"I would say that. You've seen it. It's occupied now. But when you're through with law school it will become vacant for you. It will be all yours."

"That's how Grandfather did it with you. Didn't he?"

My father nodded.

"That's how he did it."

"Why don't we finish our meal?" my mother said.

My father turned to her gently. He was always gentle with her.

"We will, Ruth. Let Pete finish what he has to say. Now is as good a time as any to hear him out."

His gentleness wasn't put on. There was no condescension in it. He really loved her and went out of his way to show her his love for her.

"Thanks, Dad."

"I assure you, you are welcome."

He could be sarcastic when he wanted to. Cut right through you. In a very quiet, controlled manner. And I guess, when it came to him, I could be that way, too.

"I like baseball," I said. "Maybe I'll stay with it."

"I see."

"Maybe I'll stay with it."

He reached over to the decanter and poured a glass

of wine for my mother and then silently handed it to her. Then he poured himself one.

He waited for my mother to sip her wine and then he sipped his. He set down his glass and looked across the table at me.

"Pete," he said quietly. "I don't want to hear any more nonsense about making a career of baseball. Is that clear to you?"

"It's clear."

He smiled, a kind of cold smile.

"You can play it as long as you wish. When you go to Princeton you can play for their team. I understand you have quite a talent for pitching."

"I've been told that."

"You'll certainly make the team."

"There's a good chance I will."

"You're free to play as long as you wish. At Princeton."

He sipped his wine once more. I waited till he set the glass down. I watched the play of light on the crystal and then I spoke again.

"So I'm to go to Princeton?"

"You always knew that."

"That's true. I'm to go there as you went there and your father before you and your father's father before him."

"If you put it that way."

"It's a fine school," my mother said. "One of the best in the country."

"Yes, Mother. I know that."

"We only want the best for you, Pete."

"I know, Mother. The best."

"Pete," my father said sharply. "Don't patronize your mother."

"I'm not," I said.

I wasn't. Even though it sounded that way. I truly loved her, all the way. Because it was easy to love her. She was so open and vulnerable. All she ever

22

wanted from life was peace. Peace for everybody she ever came to know and like.

I never once had a bitter word with her.

"Then the subject is over with," my father said.

I shook my head.

"Not at all. I hear you quite clearly but I'm not going to listen to you."

And I got up and left the table.

4

I walked slowly over to the playing field and had a catch with some of my friends, and then they left and I turned and sat down on one of the long wooden benches and thought for a while.

It was evening and the sun was beginning to slowly go down the sky. Slowly and peacefully. I looked down one of the rows and there she was.

I got up and walked over to her.

She was sitting, head hunched over, sketching something on a large white pad. I stood there waiting for her to look up.

She was working with pastels.

"You're standing in my light," she said.

"Oh."

I moved to a side, out of her range. But I was still close to her.

"Sit down until I'm done," she said.

"Okay."

I sat down beside her.

"You're too close to me. Move a bit away."

"Sure."

I moved a bit away from her.

"Now don't talk for a while."

"Sure."

"Stop saying sure. Think of another word."

"Okay."

"That's just as boring. Use your mind."

"Sure."

And all the time she was working away at the pad. And now I could see she was sketching in some pink clouds floating over a cluster of dark trees that stood at the far end of the playing field.

She was quite good.

The sunlight glinted off her hair, little golden tints, and she had a lovely scent to her. I sat there and looked long at her profile and I didn't say anything.

After a while she sighed and set down her chalks.

"I've had it."

"Looks pretty good to me."

She turned and looked squarely at me. Her eyes were large and blue. Very steady eyes.

"Know anything about art?"

"I like it."

"I didn't say that. I asked you a question."

"I like it and I know it."

"Whom do you like?"

"Whom?"

"Answer the question."

I was listening to the voice. To the low, throbbing tone.

"Well?"

"Oh. I like Rembrandt. Cézanne. The Impressionists."

"Van Gogh?"

"Very much."

"How about the women painters? Don't they exist?"

"Of course they do."

"Well?"

I thought awhile and looked at the long golden hair and the eyes that were piercing into me.

"Mary Cassatt," I said.

"Go on."

"Georgia O'Keeffe."

"Good."

"Grandma Moses."

"Keep on."

"Peggy Fleming."

"She's an ice skater."

"That's right." I smiled. "I just thought I'd throw her in."

"Just to be smart."

"No. Just to be pleasant."

Her eyes were still studying me.

"How about Käthe Kollwitz?"

"Never heard of her."

"I thought so. She's considered one of the best."

"Then I'll do my best to find out about her. Okay?"

"Okay. Then we can be friends."

Later on she told me she had deliberately come down to the playing field to meet me. It was all set up.

But I didn't know it then.

Didn't know it at all.

"I'm Pete," I said.

"Alice."

"We're in the same class," I said.

"Which one?"

"Mr. Palmer's."

"I didn't see you there."

"I'm sitting right opposite you."

"Didn't notice you at all," she said.

"I noticed you," I said.

She was putting away her art stuff into a large canvas bag. She stopped and turned and smiled at me.

It was an open and warm smile. Seemed to make her eyes larger and put a little more blue into them.

"Did you?"

"Yes."

"And?"

"I liked what I saw."

She tossed her head and her hair flashed in the dying sun.

"Cut it with that sweet talk. I don't like it."

"It's not sweet talk. You asked and I told you."

"Told me what?"

"That I... I liked what I saw."

She could fluster the hell out of you when she wanted to.

"Sweet talk is phoney talk. And I don't go for it."

"It wasn't sweet talk. It was truth."

"Truth I go for. But it was sweet talk. Admit it and let's move on from here."

I shrugged my shoulders.

"Okay," I said. "It was sweet talk."

"Okay with me," she said.

"I'm Pete."

"You told me that already."

"Oh."

"I'm Alice. In case you've forgotten."

"I haven't forgotten."

"Good," she said softly.

She could do a lot of things with that voice. An awful lot of things.

She got up and I rose, too. I was almost as tall as my father and she came to my shoulder. No more than that.

She wasn't beautiful. No, I wouldn't say that of her. She had nice features and they came together nicely. Her hair was her best feature. The way it caught the sun and glinted, in tiny golden streaks.

But I've sort of said that before. It's strange how certain little things stay with you and stay with you and stay with you and will not go away.

Her hair.

And she had kind of a pigeon-toed walk. No, that

doesn't say it at all. Her two feet sort of pointed in when she walked. No, that doesn't do it either. It was a distinctive walk. I could spot it a mile away. Because it...it had its own sweet grace.

Ah, that does it. Its own grace.

I began to walk beside her.

"Are you going to be an artist? Later on?"

"You mean give my life to it?"

"Uh-huh."

She shook her head.

"No. I just like doing it. I guess I'll do it all my life. And get kicks from doing it."

"You've got talent."

Her eyes flashed.

"Cut that sweet talk."

"Can't I give you a compliment?"

"When it's honest."

"And this is not honest?"

"No. And I don't like the name Pete."

"Why not?"

She tossed her head and her hair swung about.

"Just don't like it."

"Give me a reason."

"Reason?"

"Yes."

"There are no reasons. You either like something or you don't. I favor the color blue when I paint and I abhor the color brown. Tell me why?"

"Why?"

"Well, tell me."

"I don't know."

"You're sure?"

"I'm sure."

She nodded decisively.

"There. You see."

I really didn't see but I nodded.

"Yes."

We walked on.

"Everybody calls me Pete," I said.

"That's how it is with everybody. It's not that way with me."

"Just don't like it?"

"No."

"Why?"

"Now you're a squirrel in a cage. Get out of it."

"Okay," I sighed.

We walked on and I felt good. Very good.

"What is your name?" she suddenly asked.

"My name?"

"Your true name? Your full name?"

"My first? Or my last?"

"Your first name."

"Peter, of course."

She stopped and looked up at me.

"Nothing is ever of course in life. That's the first lesson you have to learn. You'll never grow up unless you realize that nothing is of course."

I shrugged.

"Okay."

"You got it?"

"I have."

"Good."

I learned later on that she was right. Nothing is of course in this life. Nothing at all.

We started to walk again.

"Then Peter is your name?"

"Right."

"Peter," she said again and was silent.

"It couldn't be Michael or Joseph or Alfred if people call me Pete. Now could it?"

"Quiet," she said. "I'm thinking."

"Okay."

And I was quiet.

We were walking down a lane of trees, and the fading sun fell upon the leaves and burnished them.

Then a soft breeze came up and I saw her hair rustle ever so gently.

Then I saw the leaves flutter in the gentle breeze, flutter like little bells of soft gold. Flutter and tinkle quietly.

I swear I could hear them. I swear it.

Somehow I felt I was walking in a strange, far-away world. I seemed to hear faint, lovely sounds, and nothing more than that.

All was so distant and faraway. All was so quiet and serene about me.

We walked on and we both didn't speak for a long, long while. I remember that so well, so very well. Each and every instant of the first time I ever walked with her is so clear before me. So clear and gentle.

Oh, that strange, strange quality of that fading evening. Can it ever come back? Or was it a once-in-a-lifetime shot?

I heard her voice.

"If Peter is your name that is what I'm going to call you."

"Pete is out?"

"Kaput."

"I never liked Peter," I said.

She turned to me.

"I'm sorry for you. Really sorry."

"Are you?"

"Yes."

And I could see that she was. But there was nothing she could do about it. She didn't like Pete and there was nothing she could do about it.

Maybe in her childhood she saw a cartoon on television and the rabbit's name was Pete instead of Peter and she got to hate the rabbit.

And then the name.

I don't know. I never did find out why.

I looked at her and tried again.

"My folks called me Peter."

"And?"

"When I got old enough I stopped them."

"And now?"

"They make sure to call me Pete."

"They have every right to call you Peter. They're the ones who gave you the name."

"And how about my rights?"

She shook her head decisively.

"No."

"Why not?"

"There's no reasoning with likes and dislikes," she said.

"None?"

"None."

I was quiet for a while.

"If you're so sorry why not change your mind?"

She shook her head.

"It's Peter."

"And that's how it's going to be?"

"Yes."

We walked a little farther along and I scratched my head and sighed.

"If that's what you want," I said.

"That's what I want."

And she never called me anything but that.

5

It was the strangest thing in the world. In class she never looked at me, nor ever noticed me, nor ever smiled at me. Not for an instant. She would sit there and just concentrate on what Mr. Palmer was saying, and then she'd either get into a hassle with him, or some times, and they were rare, agree with him.

The two seemed to get along wonderfully. And I had the feeling that if he could swing it some way, he'd flunk her so she could come back the next year for another round. I'm sure that happy thought kept him up nights.

But with me? Nothing.

She once dropped a sheet of paper onto the floor, and I bent over and picked it up and handed it to her, and she looked at me as if I had just come in from outer space with E.T. Looked at me and murmured a distant thank you and that was it. Didn't know me at all.

But once out of school she changed. Then she'd smile at me, a warm, happy smile, and we'd walk home together.

And it was on one of those walks that she said to me, "We're both only children."

"What do you mean?"

"Well, you're an only child. Your parents only have you. That's what I mean."

"Oh."

"And as for me, it gets a little complicated."

"How?"

"This is my mother's third marriage. And my father's second."

"Oh. I see."

Her eyes flashed.

"You see nothing yet."

"I'm trying to."

"Listen."

"Okay."

I waved my hand to one of my teammates who was passing by and then I turned back to her.

"I'm listening," I said.

"Good. Now, I have two half brothers in Tom Landry's Dallas and two half sisters in Tony Bennett's San Francisco."

"Go on."

"Two from my mother. Two from my father. Fate is evenhanded with me. Two and two. Like the animals in Noah's Ark."

"Uh-huh."

"Don't uh-huh me. Just pay attention."

"I am, Alice."

She shook her head.

"Not when you uh-huh me, Peter. Then I know you're thinking about tomorrow's game and how you're going to pitch it."

"Not at all. Not by a long shot."

But she was right. Part of me was thinking about the game. It was going to be a tough one. And it bothered me.

"Don't cozycozy me."

Every now and then she'd come up with an expression she had invented all on her own.

"What?"

"You know what I mean."

"Like Tony Bennett's San Francisco. Yes, I guess I do."

"All right then. Just listen."

"I am."

"Okay. You are."

She had stopped and her large blue eyes were staring up into mine. I felt a gentle tingle go through me. Then she turned away and started walking again.

I stood there on one spot, not moving, just watching that graceful pigeon-toed walk of hers, and then I ran and caught up to her.

She started speaking as though I had never left her side.

"I've never seen any of them."

"You mean your brothers?"

"They're not my brothers. They're my half brothers."

"And you've never seen them?"

She shook her head.

"Not even once."

"And your sisters?"

"My half sisters."

"Your half sisters."

"Never."

"How did that ever happen?"

"How do I know? That's how the cookie crumbled. Now do you understand?"

I didn't.

"Yes," I said.

"Never saw any of them."

"Do you think you ever will?"

"Ever will?"

"Uh-huh."

She spread her hands wide.

"¿Quién sabe?"

34

I nodded my head wisely.

"That's true. *¿Quién sabe?*"

We walked to the corner and waited for the light to change.

"And that leaves me as an only child. Now do you understand?"

"Yes," I said.

I figured I'd throw a lot of fastballs tomorrow and that should hold down their power hitters.

Fastballs.

Then I turned back to the problem of only children.

"Yes," I said. "This is my mother's second marriage. But there are no children from her first."

"You're sure of that?"

"Positive."

She studied me thoughtfully. Her lip puckered.

"That's what I figured. So that leaves you as an only child."

"Right."

For some reason I felt proud of the fact.

"I'm an only child," I said again.

The light changed and we crossed over to the other side.

"And that means, Peter, we're both rotten."

"Rotten?"

"Spoiled rotten."

"Why's that?"

"Because only children are always spoiled rotten by their parents and by life."

"Always?"

"Always."

"What do you mean by life?"

"It's simple if you take the time to figure it out."

"If I take the time."

"Yes."

"And you say this happens always?"

"Beyond any doubt."

"You've done research on this?"

35

"I've thought about it and observed people and then come to important conclusions. Thought about it a lot."

"But that's not research."

"I consider it so."

"But it's not, Alice."

"It is."

The sky was pink and soft about us.

"You're dogmatic, Alice," I said.

"When I see a truth I stay with it."

"That's being dogmatic."

"It's not."

I kept looking at her. Her skin was smooth and glowing in the golden light.

"Well, Peter?"

I didn't speak.

"It's not dogmatic," she said doggedly.

I was about to fight her on that but I kept my peace.

"Okay with me," I said. "We're both rotten."

"Spoiled rotten."

"Exactly."

"Good. Then we've got this thing settled," she said.

We started to walk again.

"It's been bothering you, Alice?"

"Yes."

"But now it's settled."

"For once and for all."

"I'm glad to learn that," I said.

"We're only and we're rotten," she said. "I see a great future ahead for us."

We stopped again. I looked down into her eyes.

"You do?"

"Yes. And by the way, in tomorrow's game you'd better lay off throwing a lot of fastballs."

"What?"

"Use your slow stuff and mix in some inside low curves or their power hitters will slaughter you."

I stared at her and then we walked on into the sunshine.

The next day I started throwing hard fastballs and she was right, they were killing me, and then I shifted to my slow stuff and she was right again.

We won the game.

6

Her father had been an advertising executive in Chicago. His firm moved him to New York City to head the branch there, and that's how they wound up buying a large frame house in Westfield, Connecticut.

It was an easy commute into the City and the community was the kind they wanted to be in. Upper middle class and excellent schools and a first-rate country club. They both played golf religiously. They went to the golf course more times than they went to their church. But that doesn't say much about them, lots of people do that. They had had years of instruction from golf pros and they were pretty good, but Alice took them on once and beat them, and then she gave up the game forever.

"I stood it as long as I could," she said. "And then I decided that it's a snob's game."

"You're wrong."

"For the rich, the near rich and those who like to pretend they are rich. I'm not wrong."

"Lots of people are playing it."

"Still, it costs money and time. Things the poor don't have too much of. Unless they're out of work."

"How about baseball?"

"Baseball is a people's game. You get a glove and a ball and a bat and you're in business for as long as you want to be."

"You're a people's person."

"Check."

And she was, all the way down the line.

The house was a restored Colonial, and it was much too large for three people, but they didn't seem to mind that at all.

When I say "they," I mean Paul and Ellen Cobb. As for Alice, she couldn't have cared less.

She once said to me, "I would have liked to live in Greenwich Village. In fact, that's where I'll finally end up."

"Why?"

"I like the life-style there. I don't mean the weirdos. I mean the rest of the people there. Most of the people there. Intelligent, intellectual and decent. Decent. They don't try to score off each other. They don't try to hurt each other. Yes, I think I'll end up living there."

"You mean when you get married."

"No. I'll never get married."

"Never?"

"I'll have lovers but no marriage."

"Oh."

"There you have it."

"Yes."

"You didn't like what I said."

"Didn't say anything."

"Your face dropped."

"Did it?"

"Your eyes got kind of sad."

I changed the subject. "By the way, rents are getting very high in the Village. Lots of places are going condo or cooperative."

"So what?"

"You'll have to buy to get in."

39

"Then I'll buy."

"Two and three hundred thousand. That's a lot of money."

"I'll get a lot of money."

"And your principles?"

"I'll keep them, too."

"That's a tough juggling act, Alice."

"I'm a great juggler, Peter. How in the world do you think I survived up till now?"

But this conversation took place farther on in our relationship.

Now I stood on the porch of her house and rang the bell. It was late afternoon and it was raining.

Her mother came to the door and opened it.

"Yes?"

"I'm Peter Martin. One of Alice's classmates."

She had been sick and hadn't been in class for three days already.

"Oh. Please come in."

She didn't look at all like Alice. She was tall and slender and was quite attractive in her own way. Kind of sleek and poised, I would say. But there was a sort of nervous and evasive look in her eyes.

Not at all like Alice. Alice always looked at you squarely and saw right through you. And standing there before the mother I just couldn't see for the life of me how the two of them matched up.

So I had to ask to make sure.

"Are you Alice's mother?"

"Yes, of course."

"I thought so." I smiled. "Mr. Palmer gave me some material to give to her."

"Mr. Palmer?"

"One of our teachers."

I knew then that she and Alice lived in different worlds. No, I didn't really know it. I kind of sensed it.

She stood there and gazed at me.

"Alice said you're short and plain. But you're not

40

that at all. You're quite good-looking. Tall and very good-looking."

I glanced away from her and put my umbrella in the stand. I didn't say anything to her.

"Let me tell Alice you're here."

"Okay."

"Why don't you sit down and make yourself comfortable, Peter?"

"Sure."

She led me to a chair in the living room and then went out. I sat awhile and stared out through the high windows at the rainswept lawn. And then past that to the tree-lined street. The trunks of the trees were black and glistening.

A car swished by and then all was silent again.

"She's upstairs in the first room to your left."

"To my left."

"That's it. She's eager to see you."

I smiled at her and then went up the carpeted staircase onto the landing and turned to my left and knocked on a half-open door.

"Come in."

The voice was faint and weak. I went into the room and saw Alice sitting up in a white bed, propped against white pillows. The room was high and white, and Alice's honey-blond hair flowed over the pillows.

"Hello, Peter. I feel like Camille today. You can come and touch your lips to my burning forehead. But only that."

Even the long, filmy curtains were snow white. When Alice went for a color she went all the way.

I bent over and kissed her gently on the forehead. Just brushed my lips to it. It was not burning at all.

But a thrill went through me. I had never kissed her before.

"That felt nice, Peter. Nice and cooling."

"It was."

"You're therapeutic."

"I'm glad."

41

She pointed to a small white upholstered chair. I went over to it.

"You sit over there so you don't catch my tuberculosis."

I started to rise from the chair.

"Tuberculosis?"

She waved her hand impatiently at me.

"I told you I feel like Camille today. She died from TB."

"Oh."

And I sat down again.

"Poor, poor thing," she said.

"Yes."

She sat a little farther up in bed and daintily straightened her pillows behind her.

And all the while she was speaking.

"Life can be so cruel. So desperately cruel. She had every right to have her happiness and then along comes that TB. Today she'd be up and at them. Right in the arms of Robert Taylor all the time. It's not fair, Peter. Not fair at all."

I nodded sympathetically and said nothing.

"Modern medicine would have saved her. Right, Peter?"

"Yes," I said.

She was now satisfied with the pillow arrangement and she sat back quietly. Just looking at her put a warm feeling in me.

"I was watching Greta Garbo in *Camille* last night. Did you see it? It went on at midnight. Wasn't even scheduled. I turned the dial and there it was. Did you see it, Peter? I sort of felt you were watching it with me. Did you?"

"I was asleep," I said.

"Asleep? How could you?"

"I didn't know it was on, Alice."

"You should have sensed it."

"I didn't sense it, Alice."

She tossed her head.

"It's a shame. I should've phoned you to watch it."

And she would have. And I'm glad she didn't. My father would've busted a gut, hearing the phone at that hour and it being for me.

"The next time it's on I'll make sure to phone you, Peter."

"Sure," I said and silently prayed that it never went on again.

"It's such a sad, sad story. You know it, don't you?"

"Yes."

"You ever see it before? With Garbo?"

"About three years ago."

"Did you like it?"

"Very much."

"Did you cry?"

"Men don't cry."

"But they should. They should."

She nodded her head vigorously at that. Even in the dim afternoon light her hair shone. I remember that so vividly.

I remember everything. Everything that had anything to do with her.

I wish I didn't.

"I keep my tears inside," I said.

She pursed her lips and sighed.

"That's bad. Very bad."

"Why?"

"Never repress, Peter. Always remember that it was I who said it to you. Never repress."

"Uh-huh."

"Repeat after me. I do not believe in the repression of true feelings."

"Right."

"Say it."

"Must I?"

"I wish you would. It's for your own good."

"Okay. I do not believe in the repression of true feelings."

"It will come on again. It always does," she said.

"What will come on again?"

"I'm talking about *Camille,* Peter," she said almost sternly, as if I had fallen asleep on her.

I never could get used to her shifting gears so fast. But that's the way she was. She never changed.

"Oh," I said.

"But every time it gets later and later. And I haven't missed it once."

"You seem to like it a lot."

"An awful lot, Peter. The next time it comes on I'll be sure to phone you."

"You will?"

"I promise."

"You don't have to promise," I said.

But she didn't seem to hear me.

"Even if it's four o'clock in the morning."

"Four?"

"It could be then."

"Uh-huh."

"You won't mind."

"I'll be grateful," I said.

What else could I say?

"I won't let you down, Peter. I'll call."

"I know you will," I said weakly.

"I'll call till I get you."

"You'll get me."

"Good."

"I'll be grateful," I said again.

I thought of moving out of my house and going west somewhere. Because I knew I'd never sleep again from then on, waiting for that phone to ring to tell me that *Camille* was on.

A soft light came into her eyes. Into her large blue eyes.

"Just to know we're watching it together will be a joy to me. And it will be a joy to you, too, won't it, Peter?"

"A great one, Alice. A very great one."

She smiled her warm smile at me.

44

"It's good you came to see me, Peter. Very good."

"I'm glad I did, Alice," I murmured.

"You came all on your own?"

"Yes."

"You're very therapeutic."

"Thanks."

I had completely forgotten about Mr. Palmer and the material he had given me for Alice. He was quite concerned about her and wanted me to be sure, very sure, to give her the stuff so she wouldn't be missing out on the course.

But I had forgotten all about him. I just sat there and looked across the dimness at Alice. She glowed in the soft light.

We didn't speak.

Suddenly she smiled a serene smile and settled back onto the pillows again and gently closed her eyes.

The golden silence came in again.

"I'm dying," she murmured without opening her eyes.

"Are you?"

"Yes."

Then she murmured again.

"Lower your voice. It breaks the mood."

"Okay."

"Speak very quietly if you have to."

"Are you dying like Camille?"

"Exactly."

"Oh. I understand."

"Quiet."

I didn't speak anymore.

The room became silent again, and now all I could hear was the touch of the gentle raindrops as they fell onto the windowpanes. Just that and nothing more.

"I'm dying."

Alice's face became white and composed.

"Dying." And this time her voice was almost a whisper.

And then from downstairs, as if on cue, the tender playing of a piano began. I guessed it was Alice's mother. She was playing a sad Chopin nocturne.

I sat listening to the slow, mournful music and looking at Alice's face. It gave me great pleasure just to look at her.

The lips barely opened and I heard her voice.

"When I am dead you can come over and kiss me softly. Very softly."

"Okay."

"If you can get yourself to cry a few tears, it will be just beautiful. Silent tears, if you will, Peter."

"I'll try but I don't think I'll manage them."

"Try anyway. Armand did and he was a man."

"Armand?"

"Camille's lover."

"Oh."

"You'll try?"

"Yes."

"You promise?"

"I do."

I sat there and watched Alice slowly and surely die. It was all very beautiful.

Downstairs the music began to fade away. Soon there was complete silence. Even the rain seemed to pause and wait. The windows were streaked as with tears. Silent tears.

Then Alice murmured so softly I could barely hear her.

"I'm dead."

I went over and kissed her, and this time it was on the lips.

7

I stood at the window of my dorm room and looked out at the bleak snow and thought of Alice. A figure walked past the cluster of silent trees and for an instant I could swear it was Alice, but then the figure disappeared into the veils of snow and I knew that it wasn't.

I looked down at my watch.

It was four o'clock.

Just two more hours left.

8

It seems I had kind of scared my father when I told
him I was going to make a career out of baseball
because one morning he came over to me and asked
me to come into town with him.

"Into New York?"

"Yes, Pete. I'd like you to spend the day with me
and meet a good friend of mine."

"I'd like to, Dad. But I've got a heavy schedule at
school."

I really didn't, but I didn't want to kill a day going
into the City with him.

"You could pass up a session, Pete. You do so well
with your schoolwork that I'm sure you'll catch up
in no time."

I thought of Alice and how we had planned to go
down to the Sound after school and take out my boat.
The folks had given me a ketch for my eighteenth
birthday and the weather was just fine to take it out
for the first time this season.

"Maybe some other day," I said.

"I wish you'd come with me."

I shook my head.

"We'll have to make it another time. I'm sorry."

He started to turn away but then my mother got into the act.

"Please go, Pete."

"But, Mom, I—"

"I know it's such short notice. But your father and I have been talking this over and—"

"Talking what over?" I cut in.

She was flustered. And I felt sorry for her right off. You speak directly to her and she gets flustered and hurt. Her face turns red, her hands flutter and a poignant look goes into her eyes. And it's that look that gets to you.

"About your career, Pete," my father said.

"Oh, that again. I wish you'd lay off that."

My mother put her hand on my arm.

"Please go with Dad."

"But, Mom...."

"Please."

I told you how I felt about her. And she never really made any real demands on me. Sort of let me have my own way most of the time. Even went to bat for me time and time again with my father over the years. Didn't miss a home game that I pitched in, even though to this day she doesn't know the difference between a plain curve and a slider...and now there she was with that pleading look in her eyes and he standing apart from it all, knowing that she was his big gun....

"Pete?"

There was that quivering tone in her voice. And it wasn't put on. Not put on at all.

"All right, Mom," I said.

"Thanks."

And she reached up and kissed me, and for an instant I thought it was Alice who was kissing me.

They both came up to the same height. Just came up to my shoulder.

On the train my father read his legal papers and

I read one of T. S. Eliot's stage plays, *The Cocktail Party*. I had read it before I had ever met Alice and I liked it very much. Even went out of my way to see a production of it. But now I found it harder and harder to take.

"A bunch of pretentious garbage," I murmured.

And yet I smiled because I knew it was Alice's influence on me that was doing it. And I kind of liked her having such influence on me and my thinking. Liked it a lot.

And then I remembered with a start that I hadn't called her to tell her that I wouldn't be in school and that we wouldn't be able to take that sail on the Sound, and now there was no way to get in touch with her. No way at all.

"Darn," I muttered.

"Anything wrong?" my father said, glancing up from his papers.

I shook my head.

"No, Dad."

"Are you sure?"

"Yes."

He looked at me with one of his piercing looks and then went back to his papers. They say that in his younger days he had been a trial lawyer for the firm and that he was one of the best around. Sharp and cold as ice in reading through you. A hostile, lying witness had no chance at all with him.

I guess he read through me.

But he didn't say anything.

He could keep things to himself when he wanted to. But he didn't seem to want to when he showed me around his suite of offices and had me meet his junior partners and the rest of the staff. I had been there when I was much younger. But now it was as if he was introducing me to them as a new and very important member of the firm.

And I could see from his pride in me, and I knew

then what I always knew deep inside of me, that he loved me very much.

"My son, Pete. You'll get to know him quite well in future years."

And then he said to a new junior partner who had recently come into the firm, "My only son."

"Any other children, Dan?"

"No. This is all I have."

His voice dropped a note when he said that. Became almost husky, and I glanced quickly at him but it wasn't there in his face.

And I'm sure the junior partner didn't catch it at all.

That's how he was.

And he said to one of his younger lawyers who had just come up to us, "My son, Pete, who'll become an important member of this firm."

"We'll be looking forward to that day, Mr. Martin."

"It will be here soon enough." And he turned to me with a smile. "Eh, Pete?"

"I guess it will," I said.

I surprised myself. Instead of being angry at him I found that I kind of liked the whole thing.

Why?

I don't know.

And then again I do. I guess when you really think it out, it's always good to feel that you're welcomed and respected and that there's a warm, secure world all there waiting for you whenever you feel like going into it.

I guess you have to be an idiot or a cretin not to feel good at that. Look at all the people in this country of ours who are out in the cold all the time, without any letup. And their children the same way.

I felt good.

When we got back to his big paneled office he shut the door and turned to me with a smile.

"Pete, you've just given me enormous pleasure. Thank you, Son."

I didn't say anything to him. Just held out my hand and he shook it.

"I'll always remember this day, Pete," he said.

We went out to lunch with an old classmate of my father's, Judge Thomas Gorley, and I started to get a further drift of things.

We went to lunch at the old, established Princeton Club, where a lot of important and powerful people go to eat and talk and at times come to crucial decisions. Some of them came over to our table and stopped for a minute to exchange pleasantries and sort of touch base, and then they went off, and I saw what I had already known, that my father was a big man in his field, in his quiet, controlled way.

I guess if he had wanted to he could have run for some powerful political office and got it. But that was not what he wanted to do.

And what he didn't want to do, he never did.

I guess I'm the same way, when you get down to the rock bottom of me. I guess that explains a lot of things about me.

And then again, who knows why we do the things we do? I mean the really vital things that change us for the rest of our lives. Like when you come to a fork in the road and you stand there wondering and wondering what way to go. And then you make your decision and you're on your way again.

Well, why did you choose that road over the other one?

Why?

And change your whole life by doing it?

I don't know the answer.

Who does?

The two of them had their drinks, my father his wine, the Judge a Scotch on the rocks, and I had Perrier water. We sat awhile with our drinks and then the Judge started to speak.

He was a large and very impressive man. I'm six feet and half an inch, and he was a good three inches taller than me and weighed about two hundred and forty pounds. There wasn't an inch of fat on him. I'll bet he still worked out with light weights every morning. Maybe even did a bit of jogging.

He was in great shape.

He had a ruddy face and large, even features.

A smiling, likable man.

He was about my father's age and they knew each other since college days. He had played pro football and then went into law.

And that was what he was speaking to me about. Sort of curled his way to where he really wanted to go.

"Pete, I understand you're quite a pitcher."

"I've had some luck," I said.

"He's the best in the East," my father said with pride.

I looked at him with astonishment. He had never praised my pitching before to anyone living or dead. In fact, he made a point of never even acknowledging it.

Only when he was forced to.

But nobody was twisting his arm now. Nobody at all.

"That's pretty good," the Judge said.

"Some sportswriters rank him with the best high school pitchers in the entire country," my father added.

"That's really going some."

"Isn't it?"

"Could possibly make a career out of it," the Judge observed.

"He could very well at that, Tom."

The Judge shifted the ice in his glass.

"But it's a long way to the big leagues. Very few ever make it."

"I think Pete could do it."

And I sat listening to that and said to myself, parents are the hardest people to figure out. You never know where you stand with them.

Sure, I knew he didn't want me to try for the big leagues. He wanted me to go into his field, corporate law. But knowing him as I do, I knew he was speaking sincerely and with great pride, he really felt I could make it to the big time. And he never once said a word to me about that. You go figure them out. I can't.

The Judge drank and spoke again.

"Well, Pete, I had a pretty good time playing football for Princeton and then in the pros."

"What position did you play?"

"I was a lineman. Center."

"You were the best, Tom," my father said.

Gorley laughed.

"Let's say modestly I was good."

My father told me later that Tom Gorley was a highly respected federal judge who had rendered some very influential decisions in his court. A man of power and great integrity.

"I had a good time playing and then one day I said to myself, is this what I want to do with my life? I knew I couldn't play for too much longer. A few more seasons. But I had to make up my mind whether I wanted a career in sports or to go into something more creative and fulfilling in a personal and social sense. Do you follow me, Pete? Do you, lad?"

"I'm listening."

He chuckled.

"Then you're following me. For example, I had a very good offer to go into network sports broadcasting. A long-term offer."

"I understand," I said.

I was looking at a big gold ring on his middle finger. It had a small diamond and a raised insignia surrounding the diamond.

His eyes went down to the ring. He smiled and held up his hand to me.

"We won the NFL championship one year," he said.

"Oh."

I felt a thrill go through me as he said that. I don't know, if you're in sports in one way or another, it's always thrilling to meet a champion. It's hard to explain, but the feeling is always there.

"That was before the Super Bowl came in. So we were considered the champions of the football world. There was no other championship to win."

"I told you he was the best, Pete," my father said quietly.

"Yes."

A champion stands alone. Maybe that's it. He stands alone on top of the mountain and looks down on everybody else. He's made it.

I heard the Judge's low and thoughtful voice.

"Let's say I was able to grab the brass ring. Not many people can say that of themselves. But I still was not satisfied with my life. Not satisfied at all."

He paused while the waiter took away some of the dishes and then Judge Gorley began speaking again.

"So I decided to give up playing football, even though I still had some good seasons left in me. Just walk away from it and pick up my degree in law."

"Why?" I asked.

"Why? Because I'd always had a love for law. Still do. Just as your father does."

My father nodded silently.

"I have never regretted my decision. Let me put it positively. Law has been a joy to me for many years. A joy and a satisfaction."

"And you're saying I should do the same thing, Judge Gorley?"

He waved his big hand at me and smiled.

"Tom."

"Tom."

"I'm just telling you what I did, Pete."

He buttered a roll, took a bite of it and then set the roll down onto his small, glistening plate. I noticed something that intrigued me. Massive as he was, his movements were almost dainty. Dainty and graceful.

He must have been fast on the field, I thought. Fast and lethal.

I had played a year of varsity football before I left it to concentrate on my pitching. And just looking at the man across the table from me, I could easily gauge his strength and power.

I'd hate to have him tackle me head on, on an open field, I thought. He must have been a pleasure to watch in action. Yes, he is a champion, through and through.

"Just telling you what I did," he said again.

"I get it."

"It was a good decision, Tom," my father said.

The Judge looked at him and nodded.

"It was," he murmured.

We were silent for a long while, eating through our meal. I was thinking about him and trying to picture this big man sitting in his court, and judging a case. How impressive his presence must be. He must control the show from the word go.

It must be a great feeling to have. A champion feeling. You become God.

The Judge put down his napkin, folded it carefully with his big, expressive hands and began to speak.

"Pete."

I glanced over at him.

"Yes?"

"Are you ready for some serious talk?"

"I guess so."

"And some serious listening?"

"Sure."

He moved the napkin away from him and his hands became quiet again.

"Now listen to me, lad. I'm a man who studies deeply, sometimes on the fly if the occasion demands it, and then I come to a decision."

I waited.

"I've known your father for many years. I know what kind of a man he is. And now I sit with you and study you and come to my decision. Are you listening?"

"Yes, Tom."

"Tom. That's better. Pete, I'm going to make a promise to you. You go to Princeton and then into its law school, and every summer you're there, college and law school, you have a job with me."

My father looked at the Judge and their eyes met.

"Every summer?" I said.

Gorley nodded.

"Yes. You'll be breathing and learning law as it is lived and practiced. You'll be observing its human drama from backstage and center stage. After a while I'll even be discussing my decisions with you and showing you how I came to make them."

"It sounds like a great opportunity," I said.

"It is," my father said. "You've no idea how great it is."

Gorley waved his hand at my father.

"Let's not push him, Daniel."

"That's true, Tom."

"He's got to want it himself. From inside. Like I did. Like you did."

"Yes."

The Judge turned back to me.

"You think it over, Pete."

And I wanted to tell him then and there I would take the offer. But something within me kept me from speaking.

"Take your time. And when you come to a decision you just lift the phone and call me."

"All right."

"Until then I'll hold off with anybody else."

"Anybody else?"

He smiled at me.

"I get a lot of people coming to me, Pete."

"Oh," I said.

"But you are now at the head of the line."

"I appreciate that very much, Judge Gorley."

"Tom."

"Tom," I said.

And again I wanted to tell him my decision. But I didn't.

On the way home on the train, my father was busy with his papers and I just sat there, looking out the window and thinking.

Not once did I think of Alice.

9

"You could've called me."

"I told you I forgot. And when I remembered it was too late."

"Why too late?"

"I was on the train."

"So?"

"So how could I call you from the train?"

"There are no phones on the train?"

"Alice, you know that."

"Know what?"

"That there are no phones on the train."

"There are."

"There aren't."

She shook her head and her hair swung in the sunlight, and it made me feel more guilty than ever. Just seeing that golden swing of her hair. It got me right in the heart.

"There aren't," I said again, but this time in a very low voice.

"The Metroliner has phones," she said firmly.

"The Metroliner?"

"Must I repeat myself?"

I stopped and gazed at her.

"Alice, you know well enough that I went in on the New Haven Line."

"I don't know anything well enough about you anymore, Peter."

"I went in with my father. And he always goes in on the New Haven Line. And there are no phones on that line."

"Then they should have them."

"Should have them?"

"We're in the twentieth century. Not the fourteenth. Trains should have phones."

"All right. I'll talk to the trainmaster the next time I see him. I'll remind him we're in the twentieth century."

"Now don't go sarcastic on me, Peter Martin."

"I'm not being sarcastic."

"But they come to a station. Don't they?"

I stared at her.

"Who comes to a station?"

"You're not paying attention. By the way it's not the twentieth century. We're closer to the twenty-first century."

"Just what are you talking about?"

"The New Haven Line, of course."

"Oh," I said.

We started walking again.

"Well?"

"Yes, Alice. The New Haven Line stops at stations like all trains do."

"And?"

"And what?"

"Stations have telephones," she said triumphantly.

"Oh," I said.

"Well?"

"Of course they do," I said. "Did you want me to get off the train at Stamford and phone you from there?"

"You could have."

"Could have? And leave my father on the train to go into New York all by himself? You wanted me to do that?"

She retreated.

"How about Grand Central?"

"Grand Central?"

"They have forty-one phones in that station. I counted them."

I believed she did. Why, I'll never know.

"So why didn't you pick up a phone in Grand Central Station and call me?"

"Why?"

"I'm waiting, Peter."

"You were in school then."

"I was."

"So there's your answer."

She shook her head.

"No answer at all. The school has phone service."

"I'd have to call the principal's office."

"So?"

She stopped and put her hands to her hips and gazed up at me. There were little diamond points in the centers of her eyes.

"And have you taken out of class?"

"Why not?"

"They only do it for emergencies."

"Well, wasn't this an emergency?"

She whirled about before I could answer and crossed the street against the light, and I ran wildly after her and almost got hit by a car.

A truck with an out-of-state license, no less. Rhode Island.

My father once said to me with a glint of devilish humor in his eyes, "If you have to get hit, never get hit by an out-of-state vehicle. It gets quite messy legally, Pete." And then his eyes became cold and he said icily to me, "Watch how you cross those busy

61

intersections. You make me shiver when I see you cross one."

The truck driver screamed at me and I hollered back at him, and then I caught up to her on the safety of the sidewalk.

"An emergency?" I said. "I don't think they would look at it that way."

"I'm not interested in how they would look at it. To me it was an emergency."

"Nelson would blow his top."

Nelson was the principal, and he could be tough and mean when he wanted to. And he seemed always to want to.

"Let him. Peter, you loused up my day. And that is an emergency to me. It's more than that. It's a bloody outrage."

"I'm sorry."

"Sorry doesn't help me. I wore a special white dress for our sail. And you never showed up."

"A white dress? Why a white dress?"

"Because I felt in the mood for it."

"You would have been better off in jeans."

"I just wasn't in the mood for jeans. I felt like white and I felt like silk. I do what I feel."

"Silk?"

"Silk."

"But the white silk dress would get all wet."

"So?"

"We were going on a boat, Alice. A pretty small boat."

"And?"

"The spray. The boat bounces on the waves."

"I've been on boats before. I'm no Visigoth."

"But why a white dress?"

"I told you I felt in the mood for it. And I follow my moods. Some people believe in astrology, I believe in moods."

I was silent.

"It would do you good to follow your moods. That's

what distinguishes us from the animals and the amoeba."

"Let it all hang out."

"As you put it in your crude way. Exactly."

We walked along and suddenly it came to me.

"The white dress."

"Well?"

I looked at her and smiled.

"Camille again?"

She turned and glanced sharply at me.

"And what's wrong with Camille?"

"Nothing," I said hastily. "Nothing at all."

But I had started her off again on the bitter wrong I had done her. And I could have kicked myself for doing it. Everything was starting to smooth out.

"You have no pity for the poor thing, Peter, for Camille, the same as you had no pity on me when you deliberately loused up my day."

"Are we on that again?"

But we were.

"We never left it."

"I didn't deliberately louse up your day."

"What would you call it?"

"What?"

"Answer me. Don't what me."

"I'm trying to."

"And I'm listening."

"It was not deliberate."

"You said that already."

"Did I?"

"You did."

"It...it...it was an act of God," I said desperately.

"What?"

"It was something beyond my control."

"So you blame God for it."

"Yes."

She stopped under the shade of a huge planer tree. The sun went through the green leaves and onto her

63

face and hair, making little spangles of gold and shadow.

I wanted to move close to her and kiss her. And just as I was about to try, she began to speak.

I drew back.

"Peter, you've never told me. Just what do you believe in?"

"Believe?"

"Is there a God for you?"

"God?"

"A supreme being."

"Yes," I said.

Now where is she going? I wondered.

"And you do worship him, Peter? Or her, as the case may be?"

"In my way."

"And what way is that?"

"Well, I go to church with my parents on occasion."

"And what church is that?"

"The one on Chandler and Mayfair."

I was being careful with every word I said to her.

"The big one?"

"Yes."

"I see."

She stood there very thoughtful and very silent.

"Do you believe in God, Alice?"

I had moved closer to her again. The lights and shadows on her face made me again want to kiss her.

"You are asking a very private question, Peter."

I stared at her solemn eyes.

"What?"

"We live in a country where privacy of religious belief is a sacred right."

"But you just asked me and I told you."

"That was your prerogative."

"You know, there are times when I just can't follow you, Alice," I said.

"Good. And that is how it should be."

"Why?"

"Just don't question life, Peter. Accept it. And now that I've found out that you are religious you are not to talk to me for three days."

"Because I believe in God?"

"Yes. Then you also believe in penance."

"Penance?"

"And as you do, don't call me or talk to me or make any signs whatsoever to me in class for three full days. I have left your world, Peter."

"Three?"

And I wondered to myself why three? Why not eight? Why not eighteen? Why not...? But I decided very quickly not to touch it. Leave it alone.

"I'm sorry, Peter. It's for your own good."

"It's not."

She shook her head.

"It most definitely is."

"I'm going to miss you, Alice. Very much."

"I will, too."

"Then forget this penance thing. Let's both forget it. Huh?"

"No, Peter."

"But why?"

"Because next time you'll think at least three times before lousing up my day again."

There she was again with that number three.

I've hated that number ever since. I can't stand anything that even adds up to three. My mother once put two apples and one orange on the table, and I got up and got myself another apple and put it there into the crystal bowl so it made four. And then I realized that now there were three apples. So I got up again and got myself another apple and another orange and put them there in the Waterford crystal bowl, and then everything was fine again.

My mother just stood there silent and bewildered. I'm sure she talked it over with my father.

And I'm sure he talked it over with his shrink.

"But, Alice..."

"I'm terribly sorry, Peter. It's out of my hands."

She reached up and kissed me on the cheek, let her lips linger there, and then she walked off in that pigeon-toed walk of hers.

I stood there and leaned back against the tree. I watched her walk off.

From that day onward I have been an atheist.

My hand still stroked the cheek where she had kissed it.

10

I was sitting doing some homework for Mr. Palmer's course when my mother came into the room. It was just toward evening, just near the time when she would get into the Lincoln and drive over to the station to pick up my father.

"Pete?"

I looked up at her.

"Am I disturbing you?"

I shook my head. I was glad to have an excuse to get away from my writing. It was on Melville's *Moby Dick* and it was pretty heavy stuff. And I just wasn't in the mood for heavy stuff these days. I sort of missed the walks and talks with Alice.

Penance was lying hard on me. Very hard.

"No, Mom."

"Can I sit down?"

"Sure."

She smiled and went over to a little couch that I had in the room and then sat down on it.

And as I looked across to her, I said to myself, she is in her own way a very pretty woman.

And I wondered why her first marriage broke up.

But she never said a word to me about it.

The guy must have been a real jerk, I thought.

"I wanted to ask you how you liked your trip in with Dad the other day."

"Oh."

"He seemed very pleased over it."

"I think he was."

And then again, who knows when it comes to marriages? There are always two sides to everything. Like with Alice and me.

This penance thing is an injustice. An absolute injustice.

"Did you like Judge Gorley?"

"Yes, Mom. Very much."

She nodded approvingly. "He's a very decent man. I have met his wife, Edna, a number of times over the years, and she's a fine woman. They make a very nice couple."

"They have any children?"

My mother shook her head. "No. That's the one sadness of their life together."

"I'm sorry to hear that. I've been thinking about him these past days and I've come to like him an awful lot."

My mother's eyes brightened.

"Do you, Pete?"

"Yes."

She leaned forward a bit and her voice lowered. "Then I can tell you this. He's very impressed with you. He's phoned Dad twice just to talk to him about you."

"He has?"

"Twice."

And then we were silent.

"Pete?"

"Yes, Mom?"

"I think that eventually the Judge will begin to look upon you as a son. It will be a relationship that will be good for both of you. In more ways than one."

I didn't say anything.

"It will, Pete."

I still didn't speak.

"You'll have your place in Dad's firm always waiting for you. But with Judge Gorley sponsoring you there's no telling where and how far you might go. You'll have many, many lucrative options waiting for you, Pete."

"That's if I would want them," I said quietly.

I didn't know why I said that.

"Oh," she said softly.

Her eyes looked probingly at me. And, yes, there was a touch of fear in them, too. Then she spoke again.

"Lucrative and very satisfying. In every sense."

"How do you mean?"

"He has a lot of influence both locally and nationally, Pete. He often goes to Washington. He has important friends there."

"Yes, I guess he has."

"He's a man of great honor and integrity."

"I'm sure he is, Mother."

"He is," she said.

We were silent again.

The evening shadows began to come into the room. Long, soft shadows. They fell silently over both of us.

And now I could see how my mother would look in old age. It saddened me. And at the same time put a great and yearning pity for her in me. For I knew that at bottom she was a very scared woman. Life would become too much for her sooner or later. And she would never make it. Never.

I got up and switched on the light, and it drove the fierce shadows away from her, leaving her young and pretty again.

She smiled almost thankfully at me, as if she knew deep within her what I had just done.

She began to speak.

"It's awfully, awfully important to make the right decisions in life."

"I know that."

"Awfully important."

"Yes, Mother."

She looked over to me.

"I'm starting to bore you."

I shook my head.

"No. Not at all."

"I'm sounding silly and just repeating myself. Like any nagging mother."

"You're not. Cut it out."

"But I am."

She smiled at me and then suddenly her face changed. It became tight and grim. It was all so sudden that I stared at her, but she spoke unaware of me. As if she were alone with herself in a dark and lonely room.

"It's so terrible to make wrong decisions. So very terrible. When you make them wrong, you're always paying for them. Always and always."

And I wanted to get up and take her into my arms and say, What wrong decision did you make, Mom? Tell me. Please tell me and let me comfort you.

But I sat silent and unmoving.

"Don't turn down his offer, Pete."

Her voice was now smooth and pleasant. She had come out of the dark and lonely room.

"I'm thinking about it, Mom," I said.

"Fine."

"Thinking about it a lot."

"Am I putting pressure on you?"

"You are." I smiled.

She got up and came over to me and kissed me on the hair.

"But it's gentle pressure. Won't you admit that?"

I patted her hand. It was cold to the touch.
"Yes, Mom."
"Gentle and loving," she said.
Then she went out of the room.

11

We sat in the back of the boat together. My arm was about her and I was glad that the penance was over.

My lips brushed her hair, her golden hair. And it was then that I called her "Alice of the golden hair."

But she hadn't come down to the dock with her white silk dress. She wore an old polo shirt and faded blue jeans and torn sneakers.

And I asked her why.

"I'm in a different mood today, Peter."

"Oh," I said.

That was all. I had expected her in the dress. I had looked forward to seeing her in the white dress, the sun making it even whiter, and now I looked at her and I was badly disappointed.

"The other one is gone."

"What other one?"

"The mood, Peter. The mood. You aren't paying attention."

"Oh," I said again.

The water was calm and placid. The sun overhead, gentle and shining. There were many boats out that day.

It was a perfect day for a white dress.

When I was in penance I used to sit and look through the front window and see her in my mind's eye, walking along the sparkling green lawn, walking in a floating slow motion, gliding, simply gliding along, her hair flowing in the sun.

Funny what penance could do to a human being.

"Why gone?" I suddenly said to her.

She shrugged.

"Who can explain? It goes, it goes."

"Just like that."

"Right."

"And it won't come again, Alice?"

"I don't think so. Knowing myself."

"And then again..."

She smiled.

"Who knows?"

But I knew in my heart of hearts that it would not come again.

"¿Quién sabe, Pedro?"

"Sí."

I had seen her in dresses and she could look very, very appealing in them. And now the white silk dress was gone.

There are some things you lose that never come back again. Even if they do come back again, they come back as lost.

"You're quiet, Peter."

"Just thinking."

But there would be other dresses, I thought to myself.

It's gone. It's gone.

"And Camille?"

We were now out in open water, and the horizon was shimmering in the brilliant distance ahead of us.

There were no boats near us.

We two were alone in a vast and shining world.

"And Camille?" I asked again.

"She's gone, too."

"Forever?"

"Nothing is forever, Peter."

"Then she may be back?"

"Maybe when the picture comes on with Garbo and Robert Taylor."

"The picture."

"On television."

"Yes. I know."

My heart sank.

For I knew that that telephone was going to ring at four o'clock in the morning, and my father would come into my room and shake me and shake me and shake me—I'm a very deep sleeper once I get going—and then he would bend down and put his face close to mine and say in a cold and very icy calm voice:

"You have a phone call, Pete."

"Phone call?"

"Exactly."

"At this hour?"

"At this deadly hour."

"Who is it?"

"Camille."

"Oh."

"Then you know the girl?"

"Yes, Dad."

"Pete, you have some strangely named girl friends, I must say. Who act in some very strange ways."

"Yes, Dad. She does."

"You're smiling, Peter."

"Oh, I was thinking of something, Alice."

"Tell me."

I shook my head.

"It's just between me and my father."

"How do you get along with him?"

"Okay. No sweat."

"And your mother?"

"Oh, she's fine. Just fine."

74

"And the two of them?"

"What do you mean?"

"How do they get along with each other?"

I thought a moment and then answered.

"I think they make a good team."

"That's nice to hear."

I looked sharply at her to see whether she was being ironic. But no, it was just a simple statement of fact. It was nice to hear of people getting along with each other. Especially when they were married to each other.

"Nice to hear," she said again, and this time it was in a low and almost sad voice. And then she didn't speak again for a long while.

We passed a boat and waved to it and then we were alone again.

We were sitting in the stern, just sitting there and leaning back and feeling life just shining through us.

I kissed her golden hair and then leaned back again.

She took my hand in hers and then pressed it to her lips.

"I like being with you, Peter," she said softly.

"I like it, too, Alice."

"We make a good team, don't we?"

I nodded my head.

"Yes. We do."

A spray of water went over her face and I sat a long time just watching the sun slowly, slowly dry away the little beads of diamonds. And then her face was clear of the sparkle.

"Peter," she said.

"Yes?"

"Why do people hurt each other? Can you tell me?"

Her voice was low and haunting.

"I don't know," I said.

And I didn't. I really didn't.

Maybe I do now.

And then again...

"My mother is starting to ruin her marriage," she said.

"How do you mean?"

"She's having an affair."

I didn't say anything.

"And everybody knows about it but her husband."

"Your father."

"My father."

"Does he love her?"

"Yes. Very much. That's why he doesn't know what's going on."

"I don't follow."

"He has complete faith and trust in her. It never enters his mind."

"You're sure of that?"

"Yes."

I looked away from her and out to the horizon. And her words came back to me, "Why do we hurt each other?"

"I let her have it, Peter."

I turned back to Alice.

"What do you mean?"

"Just what I said."

"Oh."

"I faced her with it once and for all. I said, 'What's going on with you? You have three children by two men. Are you going for the record? Four children by three men? Five children by four men? What is this anyway?'"

"And?"

"And nothing. She said nothing and walked out of the room."

"But you shook her up?"

"Yes. I sure did. She got pale all over and her hands started to shake."

"You think you had any effect on her?"

"I don't know yet."

"And your father?"

"I've said nothing to him."

"Are you going to?"

She shook her head.

"Why not?"

"It would break his heart. And I'm not the one to do that to him."

"But the way you tell it, sooner or later someone else will do it. You say everybody knows about the affair."

"Then let it be on someone else's conscience."

"It's a bad deal no matter which way it goes."

"Yes."

"Sometimes these things burn themselves out and no harm is really done, Alice," I said.

"You believe that?"

"Uh-huh."

"What would you do, Peter?"

"I don't know," I said.

We looked away from each other and out over the water. A pall had come over us. But the sun was still shining. Shining ever so brightly.

And then I heard her voice again.

"Peter."

"Yes?"

"Promise me this."

"Well?"

"Promise me that you and I will..."

She stopped speaking and turned away from my gaze.

"Will what, Alice?"

But she never finished the sentence. And I never found out what it was that she wanted me to promise her. Until now when I look back upon it, I think I know.

A breeze came up and the boat bounced and slapped along the little waves, and the wet diamonds were over her face again. I sat there watching them and the clear, clear blue of her eyes. But she didn't seem to see me.

The breeze went away and the water became calm again.

"Peter."

I turned to her.

"What would you do, Peter?"

"Me?"

"Yes. You."

I wanted time to think so I stalled.

"You're talking about your father and mother?"

"I am."

"I just wanted to make sure."

"Well?"

"I don't know."

"Tell me."

"What are you going to do, Alice?"

She looked hard at me.

"I'm going to hammer away at her until she breaks off the affair."

"All right. So you know what you're going to do. Why ask me?"

"Because I want to know what you would do, Peter. If you had to face a situation like this."

"Why?"

"I just want to know. That's all."

I looked into the sun and then slowly turned back to her. Her tense face shimmered before me.

"I think I would walk away from it all," I said.

"How?"

"How?"

"Peter, will you stop that?"

"Okay."

"Well?"

I ran my hand through my hair and sighed.

"I'd let it go on and let them resolve it. After all, it's between them and not you."

"I'm part of the outfit. Are you forgetting that?"

"True. But they're the ones who run it."

"I don't look at it that way."

I raised my hands.

"So you don't. That's what makes for horse races, Alice."

"You're being flippant."

"I'm not. Not at all."

"You're a conformist, Peter. Do you know that?"

"I wouldn't say that. I wouldn't say that at all."

But in a way she was right. So very right.

"You let things go along. And you do nothing about them."

"In the long run things straighten themselves out, Alice."

"You tell me."

"In the long run," I said, and my voice was weaker.

"Like the Nuclear Freeze. Did you sign the petition in school?"

"The petition?"

"Come on, Peter."

"I'm thinking it over," I said.

"And after we're blown away you'll still be thinking it over. Right? Floating up there in little fragments you'll still be thinking it over. Right?"

"Stop leaning on me, Alice."

"Well?"

"I'll sign it tomorrow."

"Do it."

"Okay. Tomorrow."

"The committee sits just outside the gym on sunny days. And indoors when it rains. So rain or shine you sign it."

"Rain or shine."

"Do it. Or we'll have no more rain or sunshine."

"You've made your point."

And I thought she was about to say more but all of a sudden she dropped the subject altogether.

Another boat came near and it was people we both knew, so we talked to them for a while and then we went on.

"That Claire was once your girl friend," Alice said. Claire was one of the girls in the other boat.

"How do you know?"

"I was told."

"Who told you?"

"Someone."

"Who?"

"Does it really matter?"

"No."

"Well?"

"Yes. She was once my girl friend."

"What happened?"

I shrugged. "Life goes on."

"She's very attractive."

"Uh-huh."

"And very pleasant."

"Yes."

"So?"

"I said, life goes on."

"Stop sounding like some corny philosopher, Peter. What really happened?"

"We got older and sort of grew out of each other. How's that for an explanation? Does it grab you?"

She laughed and swung her hair. "But you liked her a lot."

"Yes."

"As much as you claim you like me?"

"You're fishing, Alice," I said.

She looked squarely at me. "Of course I am. I want the truth."

I took my time before I spoke. "I like you more than any girl I ever met before," I said. "How is that?"

She shook her head and her eyes were still on me. "Stop cozying me."

"I'm not."

I leaned forward to kiss her gently but she drew away and looked straight ahead of her at the water and the sky, for a long while.

I let her alone and said nothing.

A spit of land came into sight and I started to

head the boat toward it. When we got close enough to see the stand of leafy trees on the shore I turned to her and smiled. She smiled back at me.

"Want to take a swim, Alice?"

"All right."

"The water's going to be pretty cold."

"So what?"

"Okay with you, okay with me."

"Then let's do it."

"I'll pull the boat into the shallows."

"Good enough."

When I was about to throw the anchor into the water I heard her say to me and the tone of her voice made me turn to her, the anchor rope tight in my hand.

Very tight.

"Even if you saw one destroying the other?"

She had never left her father and mother. Deep down, underneath it all, she had never left that agonizing problem.

And the stand I had taken. To leave it alone. Just leave it alone and let things work themselves out.

"Well, Peter?"

I thought.

"Even then."

"I could never do a thing like that."

"I guess I could," I said.

She looked sharply at me.

"We're two different people, Peter," she said.

I shrugged.

"Maybe we are. Maybe that's why we like each other so much."

And then I relaxed my grip on the rope and let the anchor slide down, deep down into the water.

"We are, Peter."

The sun was still blazing. We went in for a swim and the water was cold, but it felt great being there with her.

We laughed an awful lot and splashed water on

each other and chased each other like two little kids. It was a great, great time.

And yet I kept thinking of what she said. And I kept seeing the dark, sad look in her eyes when she said the words.

"We're different people, Peter."

We are.

It was as if she had realized it for the first time. And the truth had sunk deep within her.

When we got out of the water and onto the boat again, I held her close to me to warm her.

But I felt that something subtle and strange had come between us. Like a long, sad shadow.

"Let's go back in," she said.

"To the dock?"

"Yes."

"Why?"

"It's getting late."

But it wasn't late at all.

"Okay," I said.

The sun was out but it was no longer a shining day.

12

It happened. Just as I had dreaded it would happen.

I slowly, slowly opened my heavy eyes and there was my father's face shoved close to mine and there were his lips open and silent words coming out of them, and then the sound came on and I heard what he was saying.

"You have a phone call, Pete."

"Phone call?"

"Exactly."

He held his little gleaming alarm clock in his big hand and shoved it near my eyes and swung it back and forth.

The wavering figures finally stopped and focused. Four.

Four o'clock in the morning.

"At this hour?"

"At this deadly hour."

"Who is it?"

And I thought he was going to hit me with the clock.

"Camille."

"Oh."

"Then you know the girl?"

"Yes, Dad."

"Then tell her never to call at this ungodly hour again. Now go downstairs and tell her that. At once."

"Yes, Dad."

"Camille. Who in the world calls a girl Camille these days? Are her parents French?"

"No, Dad."

"Go!"

"Yes, Dad."

I went down the staircase and stumbled my way into the den and picked up the white phone. It fell out of my sleepy hands and onto the floor so I had to kneel and pick it up again.

And then I decided to sit on the floor and just stay there. It was so much more comfortable.

"Hello?"

"Peter?"

"It's me."

And for some crazy reason I felt a giant thrill go through me at hearing her voice. But I was still very sleepy.

"Peter, it's going on in three minutes."

"Camille?"

"Camille. I promised you I'd let you know."

"Yes, Alice. You did."

"You'll never forget the emotional experience."

"I won't."

"It's on channel three. Put it on."

"Okay."

I yawned and still sat on the floor. My eyes started to close.

"Peter."

"Yes, Alice?"

"What did I tell you to do?"

"What?"

"Peter, put *Camille* on."

"Okay."

"Now. At once. Time is racing on."

I slowly rose to my feet.

"I'll wait here for you to put it on, Peter."

"Sure, Alice."

"Hurry."

"I am."

I put down the receiver and went over to the television set and finally found channel 3 and turned it on.

I sleepwalked back to the phone and picked it up again.

"It's on."

"I can hear it."

"Good."

"But it's much too loud. Better turn it lower, Peter."

I nodded.

"You're right. It'll wake up my folks."

"Lower, Peter. It makes for a more intimate and loving mood."

"Okay."

"Go on now, Armand."

"Armand?"

"Go."

I went back to the set and turned it lower, and then I looked up and there was my father standing in the doorway of the den and my mother just behind him. Both staring at me.

I waved to them and went back to the phone.

"It's lower."

"Good. Now just sit and watch and I'll sit and watch."

"Okay."

"And keep the phone open."

"Why?"

"So we can speak to each other during the commercials."

"Okay, Alice."

I sat down and started to watch *Camille*.

And soon my father and mother came into the room and sat in their chairs and began to watch with me.

And when Camille died I saw tears in my mother's eyes, a mist in my father's, and I had a very big lump in my throat.

13

I sat at my desk and I tried to study but I couldn't.
I looked at my watch. It was five o'clock.

Outside it was still snowing.

Nobody was walking past the silent trees.

I felt that I was alone in a snowy world. Alone
and locked off from all human things and beings.

And then the phone rang.

"Hello?"

"Peter?"

The same thrill. The same everlasting thrill at
hearing her voice.

"Yes, Alice."

"You studying?"

"Trying to."

"Am I disturbing you?"

I shook my head.

"No. Not at all."

"I'm sure I am."

I shook my head again. And then I realized that
she wasn't in the room talking to me. And that made
me sad.

"You're not," I said.

"I did some shopping in town."

"Uh-huh."

"And I got all wound up in it."

"I see."

"I just wanted to check up on the time."

"Oh."

"It's for six?"

"Yes, Alice. Six."

"The Princeton Inn."

"Right."

And then she said, "I love you, Peter."

And I was about to say that, too.

But she had already hung up.

14

I went into the City to see Judge Gorley. He had invited me to have dinner with him and his wife and then go to a night baseball game with him. So I stopped off at his Central Park West apartment and there I met his wife, Edna.

"This is Dan Martin's son."

"Looks a lot like him."

"More solid in the body and handsomer in the face, Edna."

"I would say, Tom. I would say."

She was a stoutish, motherly-looking person with warm, smiling eyes. They both made you feel good and easy being with them. There are people who do that to you.

"And then he has a bit of Ruth in him, too."

She nodded.

"The eyes. They're Ruth's. How is your mother?"

"Fine," I said. "She sends her regards."

"You'll give her mine."

"Yes, of course."

"The boy's hungry, Edna. Let's eat."

"You're the hungry one, Tom. With that monstrous body of yours."

"You're hungry, too, Edna. Now admit it."

"So I am. But I'll be the one to say when we sit down at the table."

"Say it then. Before the lad goes on home and tells his folks that we starved him."

"We'll eat."

It was all done with such a light, bantering touch. With such easy goodwill. And I thought to myself, this sort of thing never goes on in my house.

The apartment was one of those huge layouts that one still finds along Central Park West. And after we ate, the Judge showed me around it. We stopped a long while in his trophy room and I sat there listening to him talk about his years in college and pro football.

I found myself drawing closer and closer to the man.

And then when we sat in the box seats at Yankee Stadium watching the ball game, just sitting there quietly, rarely talking to each other, I knew that he had come into my life to stay.

"That was a bad pitch," he said.

"I thought so, too."

"What would you have thrown him, Pete?"

"A fastball on the inside."

"Why?"

His eyes were quietly studying me.

"I saw the batter flinch at an inside fastball."

"When was that?"

"In the third inning."

"This is now the seventh."

"I know."

"And you remembered that from the third?"

"Well, I'm a pitcher. A pitcher is supposed to remember those things."

He smiled.

"If he's a good pitcher."

I didn't say anything.

"And you're a good pitcher, aren't you?"

I shrugged.

"Maybe I am."

The inning ended and we sat back, warm and comfortable with each other, and it was then that he asked me.

"Do you think you would want baseball to take over all of your life?"

I thought awhile and he waited patiently.

"No," I finally said.

He nodded approvingly.

"I kind of thought so."

"It's a lot of fun while it lasts," I said.

"And it's very good for the ego."

"It is."

"But not a lifetime thing."

"No."

And I was surprised I was so sure of myself. Just a short time ago I got a big kick out of baiting my father and making him think I wanted to make a career out of baseball. I think that underneath it all I was really playing around with the idea one way or another.

Maybe it would be a nice way to live life. Maybe I would make it to the big leagues and hit it hard and good. Become a real star. Maybe...

But now I knew for sure that I didn't want it. Not at all. It just wasn't my cup of tea, as they say.

And I wondered what had made me come to this certainty. Was it my meeting with the Judge?

Or could Alice have had something to do with it?

I sat there thinking about it long after the inning had started.

"Pete?"

I turned to him.

"You just missed a great play at second."

"I was thinking of something."

"Was a great stop and an even better throw."

I smiled at him and then turned my attention back to the game.

He's watching me and studying me all the time, I thought to myself. And he does it so quietly and naturally.

Man, I would have loved to have seen him when he was playing football. What a delight just to have watched his every move on the field.

One of the Yankee officials came by and sat with us for a while, and then he got up and left.

"Now why do you think he came by, Pete?"

"What do you mean, Tom?"

There was a merry glint in the Judge's eyes.

"Why did he take the time to come over and spend some time with me?"

"Oh."

"Was it because I'm a judge or because I was on a championship team."

"Both, I would say."

The Judge chuckled.

"It's not that easy to figure out. We're a strange people, Pete. We make saints out of our sports figures."

"Saints and very rich men."

He laughed.

"True. How true."

And then later on he said in a quiet, thoughtful voice, "We're in trouble, Pete. Our values are distorted and disturbed. We close libraries and shorten the hours our museums are open because of a lack of funds. But we have money for sports stadiums and bigger and better missiles. We're in trouble."

We sat there awhile after the game was over. Just sitting there, watching the people leave the darkening stadium, and then he said to me, "It's important to sort out truth, Pete. To get to the fundamental truths of one's life. That's all that really counts when the black chips are finally down. And you had better find out what your truth is. Because if you don't, you're in great trouble."

"I understand."

"Do you?"

"I think I do."

We stood up and he put his arm about my shoulder.

"Yes. I believe you'll make it, Pete."

When we got out of the Stadium he hailed a cab and we got into it. All the way down to Grand Central Station he was unusually silent.

I didn't speak either.

We walked into the station and then we both waited at track 28 for the gates to open.

"Did you have a good time, Pete?"

I nodded.

"I sure did, Tom."

"Would you want to do it again?"

"Certainly."

He beamed.

"What team would you like to see play the Yanks?"

I thought and he waited.

"The Red Sox," I said.

"I'll get the tickets."

"Good enough, Tom."

The gates opened and we shook hands.

"Thanks for everything, Tom."

"It was my pleasure."

And he stood there, seeming to wait for something. And I was about to say to him, I accept your offer, Tom. With all my heart.

But I turned and walked rapidly down the ramp to the train. When I turned and looked back, the giant figure was gone.

15

As I look back upon it all, I wonder why I had never told Alice about the Judge and me. But then one afternoon, a late afternoon, after baseball practice, we were both sitting in the empty stands just relaxing and I sort of got into it.

The way it worked out I really didn't.

But I tried.

"I've been thinking," I said.

She turned to me.

"Of what?"

"Of life ahead of me."

"What do you mean?"

"Oh, the years ahead."

I didn't say anything more.

"Well?"

"Well what?"

"I'm waiting, Peter."

And when I saw her clear eyes on me I sort of moved away from it for a while. I don't know why I did that.

But I did.

"What are you going to do with your life, Alice?"
I asked.

"What do you mean?"

"Just that."

"Just what?"

"Well, for example, a career."

"So?"

"You want a career, don't you?"

She smoothed her dress out patiently.

"Maybe I do. Maybe I don't."

"And if you do?"

"So?"

"So what will it be?"

"You're cozying me now."

"I'm not. I'm really interested."

"Are you?"

"Yes."

She shook her head and her eyes were seeing through me. Right to the core of me. It was no use.

"You're fishing and retreating," she said.

"I'm not."

"You are."

"Alice."

She leaned closer and tapped her finger on my chest as she spoke.

"You were about to tell me something and then you shifted course on me, and it winds up you're trying to have me tell you something."

"Not at all."

She tapped her finger again.

"Yes, my dear friend. Yes."

"Alice."

"So tell me what you wanted to say in the first place."

"I've been accepted at Princeton," I said.

"So?"

"You're not surprised?"

"Why should I be? Was there ever any doubt?"

She was right. There never was any.

"And you?"

"I'm okay at Wisconsin. But I don't know if I'll go there."

"Why not?"

"I'll wait and see awhile."

"Why?"

She looked out to the deserted playing field and didn't say anything. There were shadows over the grass of the outfield. And all about us was silence.

"I think I'll go into law," I said.

She turned sharply to me.

"Why law?"

"Why not law?"

"Because your father is in it? Is that the reason?"

I flinched.

"No."

"And because his father was in it?"

"It's not that at all, Alice."

"Then what is it?"

I got up and stood on the gravel and looked down at her. Somehow I felt more sure of myself standing up and looking down at her.

"I think it's the career I really want."

"You think?"

"I know," I said.

Her eyes flashed up at me.

"I don't think you know what you really want at this time of your life, Peter," she said.

"You're wrong, Alice."

"Am I?"

"Yes."

"I'm not wrong, Peter," she said in a flat, even voice.

And then we were silent for a while.

A lone seagull flew over, white and lost, on its way back to the Sound, and we both watched it.

"Even that bird doesn't know where it's going," Alice said.

"It's headed for the open water. It does know."

"But it didn't know before. What is it doing out here?"

"It knows now."

"Because it got lucky."

"It knows now," I said again.

The gull was now gone into the waning sun. A flash of a golden wing and then nothing but the reach of sunset sky.

She looked up at me and her eyes were earnest and pleading.

"It's a terrible, terrible feeling to be lost. So many of us just lose our way and never find home again."

And would you help me find my way? I wanted to say to her.

"You've got to be sure of what's going on inside of you, Peter. There's a core of truth there, Peter. And you'd better find out what it is."

"I think I know."

She went on as if she hadn't heard me speak.

"You'd better find out. Sometimes it takes years of searching. And sometimes you just know it."

And as she was speaking I thought of the Judge and the words he had said to me about the truth. It was as if she had been sitting with us in the Stadium and listening with me to what he was saying.

"It's in my blood," I said. "Law's in my blood."

And I was surprised myself at hearing those words come from me.

She stared up at me.

"What?"

"In my blood," I said defiantly.

"Oh, that's a bunch of crap."

"Now, Alice—"

"In your blood, no less. Come on, Peter. Get off that stuff."

"It's what I said."

"What have you been smoking lately?"

"Lay off, Alice."

"You're talking like a fool."

"Am I?"

"Yes."

"A fool?"

"In spades."

I flared up at her.

"You know, Alice, sometimes you just... just...just...Oh!"

I walked away from her and out to the diamond and just stood there looking past the playing field and out to the distant trees and the stretch of darkening sky.

I was standing right on the pitcher's mound.

Now that I think back on it, it was like a security blanket to me. I always felt good and protected standing on the pitcher's mound. It cut the world away from me.

I stood there, tight and angry, and then I felt her beside me.

I looked down at her.

"Sometimes I talk too much, is that it?" she asked gently.

"No," I said.

But she nodded her head sadly.

"But I do."

My anger was leaving me fast. "Forget it."

"No. I touch nerves. Raw nerves, and I hurt people that way, Peter. Hurt them, don't I?"

"You're okay," I said.

"But I'm not. I'm not. And I hurt you, didn't I?"

"No."

"I did."

And there was such a lonely, lonely look in her eyes that it went to my heart. And I ached.

"You're the last person in the world I would want to hurt," she said.

"Alice."

"The last person."

I looked at her and then I took her into my arms

and kissed her. A soft breeze touched our faces and our hair.

Her eyes glowed.

"Peter," she said.

"Yes?"

"Let's promise each other this."

"What, Alice?"

"Never to hurt each other."

I nodded slowly.

"I go along with that."

"Say it."

"Okay."

"Please."

"Never to hurt each other," I said.

"It's a promise."

"It's a promise, Alice."

And then we kissed again.

High, high above us the gull came back, wandering and lost. We saw him but we paid no attention to him.

As I think back upon it, I wonder if he ever found his way to the open water again. Sometimes we never do. Our whole life long.

16

It's in my blood.

Now how did I ever say a thing like that? Alice was right. She saw clear through it, and that is why she lashed out at me.

Had it coming to me. All the way.

I was standing in the supermarket buying some fruit for my mother, just standing and waiting in line for the stuff to be weighed and thinking about Alice, and then I heard a low, pleasant voice behind me.

"Aren't you Peter Martin?"

I turned and saw Alice's mother standing behind me.

"Yes."

She smiled.

"I thought so. Have you your car with you?"

I shook my head.

"No. I'll walk the few blocks home."

"No need. I'll drive you. If you wish."

"Well, I..."

"Let me do you the favor."

"All right," I said.

"Good."

I carried her packages to the car and put them into the trunk, then swung the lid shut and got in beside her.

We hadn't spoken much while in the cashier's line, just casual talk, and I found her pleasant.

And now I sat beside her and saw her clear profile and her poised way of driving and talking, and I thought of what Alice had said of her.

We stopped for a light and she turned to me.

"Alice tells me you're going to Princeton."

"Yes."

"She's been accepted there, too. You, of course, know that."

I stared at her silently.

"You didn't know?"

"I thought she was going to wind up at Wisconsin. She seemed to like the whole setup out there."

The light changed and we went on.

"She does. But I think she'd rather go to Princeton."

"Why?"

Her mother glanced at me and smiled.

"Oh, I guess she likes the school and the people going to it."

I felt a warm glow start within me but I didn't say anything.

"I guess Alice could go to any school in the country if she wished. She has top marks."

"I'm sure she can," I said.

"She has a brilliant mind."

"She has."

And I thought of Mr. Palmer and how devastated he was going to be when he came into class in the fall term and looked for Alice's face and didn't find it. Would never find it there again. Never again to challenge him.

I'll bet he'll retire. Just pack it in and retire. Once

around with Alice and you never get over it. Your life is not the same after Alice.

And then I heard her mother say, as if reading my thoughts, "Alice is quite a girl."

She said it simply, without a trace of irony or bitterness.

"Yes," I murmured.

We turned down my street and I pointed out my house. Alice's mother nodded and drove slowly over to the curb. She turned off the motor and we both sat there for a moment.

"You have a lovely house and grounds," she said.

"Yes. It's nice."

"Your father is quite a successful lawyer. Isn't he?"

"He is."

And I sat there waiting. For I sensed that all the time she was preparing to tell me something.

And I wasn't wrong.

"I understand it's an old, established firm."

I nodded.

"It goes back many years. My grandfather was the one who started it."

"And I guess you'll be going into it, too?"

"I don't know."

"Going to wait and see?"

"Sort of."

She took out a pack of cigarettes and offered me one. I shook my head.

"That's right. You're an athlete." She smiled.

"I just never started," I said.

She lit her cigarette and then dropped the silver lighter back into her purse. She let the smoke come through her fine nostrils.

She is a very attractive woman, I thought. And she knows it.

A car passed by and then the street was silent again. The leaves of the trees were full and motionless. It was a soft and beautiful day.

"Does he handle divorce cases?"

"What?"

She had startled me.

"I'm divorcing Alice's father," she said.

I was silent.

"I know how close you are to Alice. And I wish you'd speak to her."

"About what, Mrs. Cobb?"

"About laying off me." She said it softly, so very softly.

"Oh."

I felt a chill spread over me.

"Alice is a realist. Alice is a romantic. Alice is many things. Many, many things all at once. Wouldn't you say?"

"She's okay."

I really didn't know what to say to the woman.

"Perhaps that's why she's so lovable. She's so many things."

"She's okay," I said again.

"She feels she can save the marriage. That's the romantic in her. But the cold realist tells her that it is all futile."

I turned and looked fully at the woman.

"She cares an awful lot for the both of you," I said.

She flinched, and that nervous, dark look that I saw in her eyes the first time I ever met her now came back.

"I know that."

"She wants to see you stay together."

"I know that, too."

"She'd very much like to see that happen, Mrs. Cobb."

And then I saw a hard line come onto the woman's lips.

"What one wants and what life wants are two different things."

"I know," I said.

She smiled thinly at me.

103

"You know and so young?"

"Yes," I said.

She snuffed out the cigarette and then took out another one and lit it. Her hand shook just a bit. Then she killed the flame and opened her grey lizard purse, dropped the lighter in and snapped the purse shut. It clicked sharply.

She looked straight ahead of her when she spoke again.

"I don't love the man anymore, Peter."

"You don't?"

"It's as simple as that. There's nothing more to say."

"I guess in that case there isn't."

She smoked and then said again, "I don't love the man. It's gone for good."

"And Alice doesn't see that?"

She shook her head. "No."

"Maybe she doesn't want to see it."

"It could be that."

"Yes. It could."

We were silent for a while. I wanted to get out of the car and into the house and away from it all.

These things are so messy and it's none of my business. Why is she trying to drag me into it? Why?

And yet I sat there and waited for her to speak again.

"You're right, Peter. Alice doesn't want to see it."

"It's hard for her to accept it."

"I know."

"Maybe that's why she keeps fighting."

"I know that, too."

"But you say it's hopeless?"

"Completely. I'm through with the marriage."

"And Mr. Cobb knows?"

She shook her head. "I haven't told him yet."

I wondered why she hadn't. And then it came to

104

me that this was a scared woman. Just like my mother. Somewhere along the line life had floored her, had put her down, and she could never get to her feet again.

And as long as Alice stood there, she wouldn't make a move. Now it was all talk. Just talk of lawyers and divorce. As long as Alice stood there solid in front of her.

I heard Mrs. Cobb's voice again.

"Speak to her."

"I don't know what to say to her."

"If you care for her, you'll find a way."

"I care for her," I said.

"Then you'll do it?"

"Will it be any good? You know Alice."

"I know her."

There was bitterness in her tone.

And I wanted to say to her, You say you know her. But do you love her? Do you really?

Or are you just another rotten, selfish person who cares only for herself?

Are you, Mrs. Cobb?

Alice is not that way at all. Alice loves people.

And you would break her heart for her.

"Well?"

Because she loves you, too.

"Well, Peter?"

I'm as sure of that as I'm sure of this hand of mine.

"What?"

"You'll speak to her?"

"Yes," I said.

"Thanks."

"I'll do my best."

"That is all I ask."

We sat for a moment and then I reached out and put my hand on the car door.

"Thanks for the lift," I said.

"No trouble at all."
"So long, Mrs. Cobb."
"Good-bye, Peter."
Then I got out of the car.

17

I didn't speak to Alice. I just walked away from the whole thing. The more I thought about it the more I wanted to have nothing to do with it.

It's Alice's mother's problem, let her work it out for herself. For better or worse.

And as far as Alice is concerned, she's well capable of handling it herself. She doesn't need my help. Not Alice.

So I walked away from the whole thing and stopped thinking about it. But sometimes it came up to bother me.

I guess Alice was right when she said we're two different people. When it comes to things like that, I guess we are.

And then again maybe I should have talked to Alice. I gave my word to her mother and I broke it. Yes. I broke it.

I rarely do a thing like that. My batting percentage on keeping my word is a real good one. And here I go and break it.

I shouldn't have said I would speak to Alice.

I learned a long time ago from my father, never

give your word easily, and when you do give it, be sure you keep it.

I kind of followed that rule all through the years.

Did I get scared? Scared of being drawn into something I couldn't handle?

I don't know.

But it all turned out this way. Alice never spoke of her father and mother, and I never brought it up. And the Cobbs seemed to stay together and nothing much happened there.

I guess Mrs. Cobb's love affair just burned itself out.

And then again, who really knows what went on behind the closed doors and shut windows of that house?

For that matter, who knows what goes on behind the closed doors of any house? We're a funny people in this country. We keep so many things to ourselves. Many significant and heartbreaking things.

Unless we're Alice. She just talks them out. Right out.

Let's see it there in the open and walk around it and examine it and put a value on it.

This above all, let's be open with each other.

And then we can find a way to love each other.

And that way we can also find out who are the villains and get them off our backs. Once and for all.

Yes, that's the way Alice is.

And yet she never said another word about her father and mother and their problem. Not a word.

I remember driving up to Princeton with her to look over the place. She had decided to go there and I felt very good about it. So we walked around the campus, spent some time in the art museum, and then we went out and strolled along Nassau Street.

We stopped before one of the store windows and looked at the display of very expensive fur coats.

I wondered why Alice was spending so much time

looking at the sleek coats and the trim manikins. I knew she didn't care about fur coats. She was against killing animals to make coats out of them. She was against violence to all living things.

"We've got to get murder out of our systems, Peter. Or we're all lost. We'll all go down the drain."

"Violence is in man."

"It isn't."

"He's born with it."

"Nonsense. He's taught it. Just like prejudice. It's taught. Are you born hating black people? Or are you taught it with your mother's milk?"

"It's in you."

"Peter, cut it out. Use your head and your heart."

"All right. Let's forget it."

"No. For your own soul, I want you to think about it. See what you feel about it. Get your feelings involved, Peter."

"Okay, Alice."

"Remember."

"I'll remember."

It's funny, the things I remember that she said to me. Practically every word she ever spoke to me.

They come back and give me no peace.

Well, so now we stood before the store window on Nassau Street, and after a while I said to her, "You seem to like those coats."

"I don't."

"Then why stand here?"

"I'm just trying to figure out why people buy them."

"Because they think they're beautiful."

"I know that, Peter."

"Well?"

"I'm trying to figure out why they do think them beautiful."

And then she turned away from the window and said, "My mother just bought herself one."

I waited for her to say more.

But she didn't.

18

I couldn't sleep. So I put on a bathrobe and went down, out into the back garden, and sat there.

The night was quiet and there was a full moon in the sky. And after a while I realized that my father had come down, too, and taken a seat.

"Can't sleep, Pete?"

"That's it."

"Anything on your mind?"

I shook my head.

"Nothing really. Just woke up and decided to come down here."

"Oh."

"And you?"

"About the same."

And I wanted to say to him, We're both cozying each other, Dad. What's bothering you?

And what's bothering me?

"Mom's sleeping?"

"Yes."

"It's a nice night."

"It is, Pete. We'll soon have summer by the feel of it."

"Looks like it."

"How's the boat?"

"Fine. Having a lot of fun with it."

"We'll be going up to Ardlen soon. We'll see about taking the boat with us, if you want."

We had a summer house at Ardlen, which was sixty miles away.

"I'll think about it, Dad."

"Or we could share use of *The Viking*. Whatever you want."

The Viking was the family boat.

I often wondered why my father had named it *The Viking*. He was not much of a traveler himself. He only went on trips when his business called for it. He had no interest in going to Europe, so we never went there. When you really got down to it, he was not an adventurer.

Why *The Viking?*

Was that some way of his saying, I'm in a groove. My whole life long. And underneath it all I'd really love to break away and adventure all over the world and do some different things and just get out of this lifelong rut?

And then I said to myself, stop it. You're starting to analyze and question like Alice does. Let it alone.

I looked across to his calm and controlled face.

"Maybe I'll take the boat with us. If it's all right with you, Dad."

"No sweat, Pete."

"It's an expense to get it up there."

He smiled tolerantly at me.

"I have the money, Pete."

"Okay, Dad. Thanks."

"No bother."

And I thought to myself, he has been generous with his money to me. And to my mother. No, he's never been tight with it. In his way he's a generous man.

And he's a decent man. He has standards of be-

111

havior that he has set for himself and that he would never break.

That's how Grandfather was and that's how he is.

All in all, I've been pretty lucky with him. Some of my friends have fathers who are real disasters.

"Dad."

"Yes, Pete."

I hesitated and then I spoke.

"I've been wanting to ask you this for a long time."

"Ask me what?"

"It's about Mom."

"Go on."

I hesitated again.

"Take your time, Pete."

"Sure."

And then I said to myself, I'd better leave it alone. But yet something inside of me kept pushing me on.

I still don't know to this day why I wanted to know. And yet maybe underneath it all I do know.

Know too well.

"If you don't want to get into it, Dad, just tell me."

He smiled patiently but his eyes were alert.

"I still don't know what this is all about, Pete."

"Mom and her first marriage," I said.

"I see," he said quietly.

"It's been on my mind a long time."

"Then speak up, Pete."

I looked across the flagstones to him. A shaft of moonlight had just fallen across him. His face was white.

"Why did it break up?"

"Oh."

And then he was silent.

"If you want to leave it alone, Dad..."

He shook his head determinedly.

"You asked. And evidently it's important to you to find out at this time of your life. For what reasons...?"

He raised his hands and then let them fall to his

sides. His manicured nails gleamed. He was a neat man. A very neat man.

"I do want to know," I said.

He turned and looked straight at me.

"Her first husband had a drinking problem. One he could not solve."

"So that was it."

"Yes, Pete. That was it."

He was silent and I waited for him to speak again. He was no longer sitting in the shaft of moonlight. Now he sat half in light and half in shadow.

"Yes, Pete. It went on and on and finally she could take it no longer. And so she packed up and left him."

"Is he still alive?"

My father shook his head, and when he spoke, his voice was low but clear.

"He drank himself to death, Pete. He was found one morning in a hotel room dead from malnutrition. That's how it generally happens."

"They drink and they don't eat?"

"Yes."

"When did he die?"

"About ten years ago."

"It must have had a terrible effect on her."

"It did, Pete. For a while we thought she was going to have a breakdown."

"As bad as that?"

"Yes. You were about eight or nine then but we kept it from you."

And I wanted to say to him, You didn't. I felt something terrible had happened. But you never told me what it was. It wasn't right for you to keep it from me. I'd rather you hadn't protected me that way.

But it's gone. It's gone.

Or is it?

He suddenly got up tall and straight, walked a bit in the garden, in and out of the moonlight, and then came back and sat down again. Slowly.

"Did she love him?"

"Yes, Pete."

"She's a good person," I said.

"She is."

And then he said something I never forget.

"The heart breaks but once in a lifetime, Pete. Don't believe anybody who tells you otherwise."

Then he sighed gently and got up again.

"I think I'll go back to bed. I'm a bit chilled."

But it was warm.

"Okay, Dad."

"You're going to stay out a little more?"

"Yes."

He stood there looking at me. And then he came over and he did something he had never done before. He put his hand on my hair and ruffled it gently, tenderly. Again and again.

"Sleep well, Son."

"Thanks, Dad."

I watched him go to the house and then I saw him turn and pause.

"By the way, how is Camille these days?"

"She's fine," I said.

We smiled at each other.

"You're sure her folks aren't French?"

"They aren't," I said.

"Good night, Armand."

He turned and went into the house.

19

Somebody went by the silent trees and then all was still and white again. The snow fell relentlessly.

And it seemed to come into the room and into my heart. The Snow. The Cold. I thought of Alice. Was she waiting for me at the Princeton Inn?

I looked at my watch.

It was five-thirty.

20

"They should take him out. Before he gives up another run."

"No, Tom. I would let him have a few more pitches."

"You would?"

"Yes."

"But why, Pete? He's lost all his stuff. One run and two men on base already. He's going too fast."

"But not gone, Tom. He'll straighten himself out. It seems to me he's getting his velocity back."

"I don't see that at all."

"Give him a break."

"Well, the manager's letting him stay in. So let's see who is right."

We were sitting in the same seats in the Stadium. I finished my hamburger and drank some hot coffee.

It was a bit chilly and it looked like it was going to rain.

"He's pulling out of it," Tom said.

"Looks like it."

He turned to me and smiled warmly when the inning ended with a strikeout.

"You've got a cautious and penetrating mind," he said. "You don't jump."

I felt a glow within. I liked it when he approved of me.

"You seem to wait things out, Pete. To think them out. Looking for the facts that are buried under some tricky illusions. You'll be all right."

"I guess I'm that way when it comes to baseball."

"Baseball is an aspect of life, Pete."

And then he just sat there, silent and thinking.

The rain came down and the game was called in the fifth inning. I had some time left before going down to the station for my train.

While we were waiting for a cab, Tom stood there and seemed to be studying me.

"I'll tell you what, Pete," he said. "I have to get some important papers from my desk. Let's go down there and then I'll take you back to Grand Central."

"All right with me, Tom."

"You'll see my home away from home."

"Okay."

The cab left us off in front of the Federal Building. We walked up the wide stone steps, between the pillars, and then stepped inside. The guards let us through, and then we took an elevator up to the third floor and got out. We went down a long, silent corridor and then stopped at an oak-paneled door. And all the time the big man at my side was silent.

He took out his keys and then opened the door, and we went in.

"This is called the judge's chamber," he said.

I don't know why, but I felt something within me start to warm and surge. Then he switched on the lights and pointed to a black leather couch.

"Make yourself comfortable, Pete."

I went over and sat down, and somehow I wished that Alice were there with me. Sitting on the couch with me and feeling what I felt in that lit and quiet room. And I said to myself, the next time I see Tom

117

I'm going to ask him if it's all right to bring Alice along.

And then I said to myself, stop fooling around. You know in your heart that Alice won't go for this. She'll say it's all an illusion. It's not what you really wish to do for the rest of your life.

An illusion, Peter.

"Pete."

"Yes, Tom?"

"I've got what I want. Let's go into the court for a minute."

"Okay."

He opened a door and let me into the dark and shadowy courtroom. For some reason he didn't turn on the lights. But he led me with sure steps to the judge's bench. And then he pointed to the chair.

"Sit in it and see how it feels."

"What?"

"Sit in it."

And then I did what he said.

"How does it feel, Pete?"

"Fine."

He stood there by my side, huge and imposing, and I thought of one of the statues that stood in front of this massive building.

The open, rugged face was still, very still. Only the large eyes of the man were alive.

I turned away from him and sat there looking down across the large and shadowy room. A feeling of awe spread over me. I imagined the room filled with people: lawyers, spectators, court attendants, and over it all the hush of authority.

I, sitting there, was at the head of it all. A captain on the bridge of his vessel. Controlling it all.

And then I heard the Judge speak, as if he were reading every thought and feeling that went through me. His voice was low and sombre.

"An old judge once told me when I first sat in this chair something I've never forgotten. He said, 'Be-

118

ware, Tom. Beware of the power that is suddenly put into your hands. You'll run it all, Tom. And nobody but the U.S. Supreme Court in Washington can tell you when you run it wrong. And sometimes even they won't do it. So watch out for the power. That it doesn't topple you and take your humanity right out of your being. Watch out, Tom.'"

"The power."

My voice was almost a whisper.

"Yes, Pete. I've sat here and made decisions that have affected this entire country."

And I remembered my father telling me that one of them had become a landmark decision.

He put his hand on my shoulder.

"How does it feel?"

"I don't know how to describe it," I said.

He nodded.

"Then you're feeling the power."

"I guess that's what it is, Tom."

He nodded again.

"That's what it is, Son."

It was the first time he had used that word to me. Son. And it came naturally to both of us.

And I suddenly looked up to Judge Thomas Matthew Gorley and saw him in a new light. Saw him as a king. A king who wanted to hand down his scepter to me. When the time was ripe and full. I was to take up where he had left off.

"It feels good," I said.

And so at the station, when we stood waiting for the gates to open, I turned to him.

"Tom."

"Well, Pete?"

"I've been thinking over your very generous offer."

"In your quiet, waiting way."

"Yes."

"And?"

"I've come to a decision."

"Go on, Pete."

119

"I'd like to take it."

"You've made my day for me," he said softly.

We shook hands and I went down the ramp to the train. When I turned and looked back the giant figure was still there.

21

I wanted to tell Alice. But I didn't.

And then I said to myself, I have to wait for the right time and situation to come up. And then we can discuss it and work it out.

We'll work it out. When the right time comes.

And then the right time came.

It all happened on an impulse.

Alice and I were riding along, coming back from the dock, when I turned to her and said, "How about going up to Ardlen?"

"What's up there?"

"We have a summer house there."

"So?"

"Let's go up."

It was an early Saturday afternoon. We had just come back from a morning swim and the weather was perfect. It was a hot June day and the sun was out strong and was supposed to stay out that way for some days to come. My father had to go to St. Louis on a business trip and he took my mother along with him. So I was alone for a few days.

"It's a nice drive up, Alice. I'll show you around. And if you want we'll drive back Sunday."

"Sunday?"

"Uh-huh."

"I'll think about it."

"All right."

About a mile down the road she said, "Stop over my house and I'll get a few things."

"You've thought about it."

"I have."

I drove the car to the front of the house and stopped. She flung open the door and jumped out.

"Pick me up in an hour."

"Okay, Alice."

About halfway up the walk she turned.

"As to staying over I'll make up my mind there."

"That's your privilege."

"And I mean to exercise it."

"I know that."

"Good."

We both were smiling.

"In an hour," I said.

"Give or take ten minutes."

"I'll take twenty."

She laughed, a low, musical laugh that went through me.

"You're in a real good mood, aren't you, Peter?"

"You put me in it, Alice."

"An hour."

I watched her walk to her house with that pigeon-toed walk of hers, her golden hair glinting in the sun, and I sighed and drove off.

22

We were in the kitchen finishing an early supper, and everything was warm and good, so I decided to open up and tell her.

But I didn't do it right off.

"Let's have our coffee out on the deck, Alice."

"Good idea."

"I'll carry the dishes and you take the pot."

"Okay."

So we went out there, set things up and then sat drinking our coffee and munching on some cookies.

For a while we didn't speak. Just sat there looking out over the broad and quiet lake. There was hardly a ripple on the water.

"It's very peaceful here," Alice said.

"Peaceful and isolated. The next house is half a mile down."

"As far away as that?"

"Uh-huh. That's why my father bought the place. He likes it that way."

She turned and looked at me with a penetrating look.

"And you like it that way, too."

I shrugged.

"I guess so."

"Come on over into life, Peter. The water's fine. Just fine."

"Come off it, Alice."

She smiled gently.

"Okay."

We sat quiet again.

"It's a lovely setup, Peter. I like it very much."

"It is," I said.

"Lovely," she murmured.

The house was set on a grassy hill, and then everything sloped away and down to a sandy beach, and from there the lake spread out wide and serene. Far on the other shore we could see the glimmering white of the houses and the massed green of trees full with summer leaves.

The sun had lost its fierce strength and was now arcing down a golden, fleecy sky. A gentle breeze rustled through Alice's hair, and I sat there watching it and saying nothing.

"Yes, it is beautiful here. Lots of color and contrast."

"Especially this time of the year."

"You ever come up here in the winter?"

"Sometimes."

"It must be great with the snow all around you."

"It is."

Out on the lake a speedboat roared into view. We sat watching it dash up a greenish white spray. Then it streaked away and finally disappeared.

"I brought along my art stuff," Alice said. "Maybe I'll do a little sketching in the morning light."

A thrill went over me.

"The morning light is a good light to work by," she said.

So she had decided to stay over. And that was her way of telling me.

"You've never tried to paint, Peter?"

"Never."

"Draw?"

"Just in art class."

She swung her hair angrily.

"Those classes are for the birds. Ruin more potential artists than they make. They should be abolished."

"I have no talent anyway."

"How do you know? You ever try on your own?"

"No."

"Ever feel like trying?"

"No."

"You're hopeless."

"I guess I am."

Everything was going along fine. Just fine.

So I waited a few minutes and then I plunged.

"Alice."

"Well?"

"I know you've been planning on spending a lot of time with me this summer."

"We both have been planning that, Peter."

"That's right."

"So?"

Her eyes were alert. Those awful blue eyes of hers that saw through everything. Especially through me.

"I won't be able to do it."

"Why not?"

"I...I got myself a job."

"A job?"

"With Tom Gorley."

"Who is he?"

"He's a federal judge. A very important man."

"So?"

I looked away from her.

"I'm going for law, Alice," I said.

"Just like that."

"No. Not just like that. I've given it a lot of thought."

"I'm sure you have."

She poured herself some coffee and then put the cup away from her with a slow and deliberate gesture. She was calm and controlled. But I could tell she was steaming inside.

"Who's been conning you, Peter?"

"Conning me?"

"Who's been giving you a song and dance that law is your life's blood? From before birth you were destined for it. Who, Peter?"

"You've got it all wrong."

She shook her head.

"I've got it all right. This judge of yours. You've been going into the City to see him, haven't you?"

"I've been to some baseball games with him."

"And he's been buddy-buddy with you, hasn't he?"

"Cut it out, Alice."

"Why? Because I'm getting too close to the bone? And it hurts?"

"No. Not at all."

She leaned forward to me.

"Peter, don't throw away your life on a bad call. It's a bad call, I tell you. A bad one."

"C'mon, Alice."

And that was all I could say.

She rose and came toward me.

"You'll get caught into it and then you'll wake up one day and say, What have I done to myself? I'm trapped. And there's no way out anymore. The money is too steady and too good. The prestige. The power. The fawning people about me. My wife."

"What do you mean 'My wife'?"

She was standing over me. But now she turned and walked away to the edge of the deck and stood there gazing out over the water and saying nothing, absolutely nothing.

"I wish you'd see things my way," I said.

She didn't turn.

And I knew what she had meant. She would never

be my wife. Never. Not if I took that road. Someone else would be.

Someone I would never love.

"I wish you would, Alice," I said again.

She stood facing the calm and golden water.

"That's just the trouble, Peter," I heard her say in a low, low voice. "I am. I am. And that's why what you're saying is tearing through me."

I got up and went to her.

"Alice," I said gently.

And she turned swiftly and was in my arms.

"Peter, don't do it."

I kissed her again and again.

Her fragrance was soft in the air about me. My heart and body ached for her.

"Let's not get into it anymore," I said. "Let's just leave it alone for a while. Let's not ruin things here."

She drew back just a bit.

"Please, Alice," I pleaded.

A lost look seemed to come into her eyes and then she slowly nodded.

"All right, Peter."

And so it was dropped.

23

We were out swimming just as darkness was coming in. The water was warm and soothing, and at first we swam close to each other, then for some reason I swam away from her and headed out.

Maybe I wanted to be by myself and sort of think things out more. Maybe I was still upset at what had happened on the deck. But when I was out there and away from her, swimming easily...

...it happened.

For the first time in my life I felt a tightening in my gut, the first time in the water, and then a feeling of fear swept over me and I knew that it was becoming a bad stomach cramp. A deadly one.

"Help me."

I tried to fight it and the more I did the worse it got.

And then I remember calling out, "Alice."

And then doubling up and going under.

"Al...ice!"

It was a scream.

And that was all.

No, there was something else. I remember these

thoughts racing through me: You fool, you went in swimming too soon after eating. And you got yourself upset. And...

The other one was: Now I'm losing Alice forever.

Forever.

Forever.

That was the last thought before the blackness closed my eyes and my mind.

23

24

"Peter."

Her voice was the first thing I heard. And her touch was the first thing I felt.

"Peter."

I could see her hair, wet, so wet, and her face and her body, wet and gleaming in the moonlit darkness.

"You've been throwing up," she said. "And then you stopped."

I just lay there and looked up at her.

"And when you stopped I knew you were going to be all right."

I tried to speak but she put her hand tenderly to my lips.

"Rest. Just rest."

Then I saw her move away from me, still on her knees, and then her head went down and I heard her sobbing.

Alice, I wanted to say. Dear, dear Alice.

It was the first time I had ever seen her cry. And now it seemed as if her very heart was breaking.

"I thought I was losing you..."

Alice.

"I'm so...tired...Pe...ter...so tired..."

I tried to open my lips but I couldn't.

"I love you so, Peter...so...much..."

I love you, too, Alice.

She couldn't stop sobbing.

Above us and all about us was silence. Complete silence. Except for the sound of her broken voice.

I raised my hand weakly to her. But she didn't see it.

I heard her say again, "I almost lost you, Peter." And then she said, "I couldn't bear that."

I tried desperately to open my lips and tell her what was in my heart. But I was too weak to speak.

And so I said nothing.

25

She drove on the way home and I sat at her side. I was still not back to myself, and it was good just to sit by her and listen to her talk.

And after a while I asked her.

"Tell me, Alice. How did you ever get me in?"

"How?"

"Uh-huh."

She glanced at me and there was a merry-sad look in her eyes.

"I never gave it a thought, Peter. I just knew that I had to get you onto that beach and get that water out of you."

"But I was like a dead weight."

"So?"

"So how?"

"I can swim, can't I?"

"You sure can."

"And I can feel, can't I?"

"What do you mean?"

"I can feel that there'd be an empty hole in my life if I left you out there in that lake water."

I looked away from her. There was a mist in my eyes.

And then she said gently, "I guess I was lucky."

"Yes."

We didn't speak for a long while.

"Alice," I said.

"Yes?"

"Alice, I'm not taking that job with Tom Gorley."

"But Peter..."

"It's not for me."

And I thought she would say something. But she didn't. She just drove on, and soon we were back home.

26

She didn't say anything because she saw the truth.
Alice always saw the truth and never walked away
from it. I always ran from it. Yes, I know that now.
I would run and hide in a corner and then wait for
it to find me out.

And yet this time I didn't run.

I had learned from Alice to fight.

And this time I did. I tell you I did.

I can say that for myself.

This time I tried my best. For I remember calling
to speak to Tom Gorley, to tell him of my new decision, but he was on his way downtown to court, so
he asked me to meet him there.

"But, Tom," I said.

I wanted to do the thing right on the phone and
have done with it.

"I have to run out, Pete."

"It'll only take a few minutes."

"Have to, Pete. I'm too late already."

"Okay, Tom," I said.

"Then you'll come in?"

"Yes."

"Good. And then we can talk and see what your problem is."

"Right, Tom."

I put down the phone and knew that I had lost the first round.

But I took the train and went into the City and then down to the Federal Court Building. I sat awhile in the courtroom and watched Judge Thomas Matthew Gorley preside in his flowing black robes. And as I sat there I felt more and more the powerful attraction it all had for me.

How easily he held sway.

He spoke little, but when he did, all was silent and expectant. All waiting on each and every word.

And then later in his chambers there was another judge there, and Tom put his big arm about me and said to the man, "This is Pete Martin. I never had a son, Jeffrey, but I have the feeling that this young man will be one."

"A fine-looking fellow, Tom."

"He is."

"Going into law?"

And before I could answer Tom was speaking.

"He's my protégé, Jeffrey."

"I see."

And he smiled at me.

"Congratulations, Pete. You couldn't find a better sponsor for yourself."

And then when the judge had left us, Tom turned to me.

"Sit down, Pete."

But I just stood there.

"What's the problem?"

"Tom."

"Yes?"

And then I shook my head under that penetrating gaze.

"It's gone, Tom."

"You sure?"

"Yes."

He stood there appraising me and then he took off his black robes.

"Since you're in town let's have lunch."

"All right, Tom."

It was a very pleasant and warming lunch. I always felt good with Tom. So very good.

But yet through it all I knew that I had lost.

My career was set. And there was no turning back anymore.

27

I found her in the playing field. She was out on the grass sketching some trees and a patch of blue sky.

I went over and sat down on the grass beside her.

The morning sun made her hair glow and sparkle. And when she turned her eyes to me they were so blue, so blue.

"I called you yesterday," she said.

"Yes. They told me."

"You went into the City?"

"Yes."

She erased some lines and then started drawing again. Her strokes were swift and precise.

She always knew what she was doing.

"I went in to see Judge Gorley," I said.

"So?"

And I said to myself, will this be the last time I shall ever hear her say "So?" to me?

Her voice rising just a bit into a lilt. Like a phrase of soft music.

So?

"I went in to tell him that I was turning down his offer."

"And?"

She still went on sketching. But I saw one of her hands tremble just a bit. Yes, just a bit.

"It didn't work out that way, Alice."

"It's a bright morning sun," she said.

"What?"

She shook her head and didn't speak.

"I didn't say anything to him, Alice."

"Oh."

And that's all she said.

"I lied to you the other day. I said I was giving up the job."

She shook her head and paused in the sketching.

"No, Peter. You didn't lie. You spoke truth then."

I looked away from her direct gaze.

"You meant every word you said. Every word. But now you find you can't live up to it. Isn't that so?"

"Yes, Alice."

"So what is one to say?" she murmured.

"Alice."

She sighed and then threw the drawing pencil away from her.

"The sun's too bright. I'm making too many mistakes. I think I'll pack it in."

I slowly got up.

"Alice, we can go on, can't we?"

She shook her head.

"No, Peter."

"But why not?"

"Peter, stop running away."

"I'm not."

"You know how I feel toward you. With me it's for keeps."

"Yes, Alice. I know."

She drew in a breath and then began to speak.

"Sooner or later you're going to realize that you've made a terrible mistake. And as I said to you, it'll be too late then to do anything about it. You'll be in too deep. Much too deep. Over your head, Peter, like

It's no use.

I went to the phone and called the Inn and asked for her to tell her that I wasn't coming. But she had already left.

I guess she knew when six o'clock came and I wasn't there that I would never come. That it was all over between us.

I sat down on my chair and kept looking at the floor. Trying not to think of anything.

And then after a long while I realized that the bell was ringing. Someone was downstairs at the door.

I got up and stood listening to the bell until it stopped ringing. And then after some minutes had gone by I went to the window and looked out.

She was standing there in the snow, her face upturned.

Our eyes met.

One long look. It told the two of us that we would never see each other again. The thought made me so cold. I began to shiver. I put my hand out but she had already turned away, and it was then that I frantically pushed up the window and opened my mouth to call out to her.

But no sound came.

Why?

I saw her walk past the silent cluster of trees, and then all I saw was the falling veils of snow.

The heart breaks but once in a lifetime, my father had said.

But once.

Once.

I never said I loved you, Alice.

JAY BENNETT has won, in two successive years, The Mystery Writers of America's Award for the "best juvenile mystery." The author of many suspense novels for young adults, Mr. Bennett has also written successful adult novels, stage plays, and radio and television scripts.

Mr. Bennett's professed aim in his young adult novels (which have sold over a million and a half copies) is "to write honest books that speak about violent times...but throughout the books, and in every word I write, there is a cry against violence."